Vivaldi's Girls

Vivaldi's Girls

D.P. Rosano

"Venice once was dear, the pleasant place of all festivity."
Lord Byron

July 29, 1741
Vienna

He now rests beneath the soft brown earth.

As I stare down at the newly shoveled mound at my feet, the notes of his last composition come back to me. I recall our meeting last night as I sat in a small chair next to the fire in his study. We chatted as if we were friends; he smiled and told small anecdotes, mostly about himself, and I had to hide my bitterness from him.

Once more I am alone with him. The gravediggers are gone; all his girls and all his bootlickers have left me alone on this little hill in the Bürgerspital Cemetery to pay my last respects. But respect left long ago; I am here to look down on him one last time.

He can no longer bother me with his arrogant stories. My mind is fixed on revenge – not the impulsive revenge that sparks an explosion of anger, but the type of revenge that is eternal. I look up at the blue sky and hope. Perhaps the angels who came for him when his breath failed for the last time recognized him. Perhaps they saw the face that the heavens had warned them about. Perhaps they then cast him down rather than lifted him up.

Last night, I stared at him in the dim light of the candelabra on the piano as his head rocked gently with the rhythm of the music. The melody that he had written was soft, mournful, and – I admitted to myself – lovely. The vibrations that rose from the pianoforte created gentle movements in the air, weaving their way toward me. His great talent had always been making each person in a room believe he was the audience for whom the music was composed.

But when I looked at Antonio and saw the thin smile on his lips, I was reminded once again that he only played for himself.

I shifted in the chair and crossed my weakened left leg over the other, settling once again just as he too shifted toward the lower register of the instrument, softly caressing the keys and gently sliding his fingers off the edge of the ivory.

I was there last night because he had just composed this new sheet of music and he had summoned me to his poor one-room flat near Stephansplatz to hear it. Antonio had an insatiable need for approval, and I supplied the audience so that he could prove that he was still the genius that the world remembered. He didn't claim it was his masterpiece, but he wanted an endorsement from someone, and I happened to be in Vienna at the time. I smiled impatiently and accepted, but I had my own personal reasons for visiting him.

For an hour after I arrived, we sat and passed the news of the day with inconsequential stories, neither of us particularly interested in such small talk but using our back-and-forth conversation as a swordsman might parry his opponent's jabs until the right opening offered itself.

The candle flickered and the short stubs of wood in the fireplace crackled. Warmth wasn't needed inside this room, not in July, but the low flames from the hearth threw off a dim and meager glow in the room, enough to light his face and the keys of the piano that his fingers rested upon.

Our talk that evening had been as one between men of an advanced age who shared memories of life and time. If a stranger had stood in his doorway that evening he would be forgiven for thinking that Antonio and I were friends. But despite our years in each other's company, friendship was not the reason we were drawn together.

The truth was that we both loved the same woman. She was only one of his 'adventures.' But she was my wife, a girl that I had loved since her birth in my twenty-first year. A young child I had watched grow into womanhood, whose sparkling eyes and long blond tresses endangered any man who caught her in his gaze.

Despite all her suitors, she chose me, a man with a gimpy leg, thinning gray hair, and many more years on earth than hers. And the miracle of it was, she loved me.

But she was also in love with the music he created. It enchanted her, and he used these sonorous tunes to lure Rachel just as he had lured other young girls into his arms.

In the end, I was the one who would have to make Antonio Vivaldi pay for his sins.

June 1693
Venice

Antonio's birth in the year of Sixteen Seventy-Eight was marked by the evil eye. On that day, there was an earthquake in the city, the first in distant memory, and his health was said to be weak from the beginning. Just out of his mother's womb, Antonio coughed and sputtered, his chest heaving in great attempts to draw in air, and his family thought he would expire before sunset on the same day. So, the midwife baptized him that very afternoon, an act condemned by the priests of Venice as insufficient and against God's will. But Antonio's mother, weakly recovering from a difficult birth, feared that the baby – now breathing – would die in her arms and go to hell without a proper baptism.

Antonio Vivaldi was born the same year that I was. His family was not as distinguished as my own; his father was just a barber.

Giovanni Vivaldi was busy trying to make money to provide food for the family and was out of the house on that day. He learned of the birth and baptism from a friend in the square.

The infant Antonio survived. He spent many years of his youth with suppressed breathing, a fate which followed him into later life. In our earlier years, as with most children, the riches of our parents seem to be only a veneer upon life itself; we didn't distinguish between those who had more and those who had less, if we were in each other's company. I sympathized with Antonio's plight, but my father convinced me that it was on no consequence for us.

"Don't mind him," he said. "He's just a musician."

Whenever I spoke with Antonio over the years, his voice always seemed to be squeezed out between breaths, sometimes almost a wheezing sound. I listened carefully so that I could catch his words, but my father's own words replayed themselves in my memory.

Antonio's father possessed some musical talent and it was this that offered some slight reprieve from the duties of serving as a barber to the moneyless class. His abilities with musical instruments were modest, enough to give his son and other eight children an opening to the world of concerts and operas, but not enough to distinguish himself in the upper class of *maestri* in Venice.

Although he sought talent in his progeny, Giovani despaired of any true musical excellence in his offspring. He believed that they wasted the opportunity – or were simply not up to it.

But Antonio was different. From an early age, he displayed an uncanny ability to perform on the violin. He was all but prohibited by his parents from learning the wind instruments; his thin breaths and harsh breathing would never have let him succeed at that assignment.

When he was only fifteen years of age, Antonio's parents offered him to the Church for a life in the priesthood. His mother was probably still in dread of the evil eye she said hovered over his life. Antonio's father was more practical. With eight other children, Master Giovanni just wanted his precocious son to find a solid career in the cloth.

By this year, Antonio had already applied his musical genius to write a liturgical hymn. *Laetatus sum* was a brilliant and joyful composition that combined exquisite orchestration with soaring vocals and seemed to bring heaven down to earth. Perhaps Giovanni's fantasies for his young son's advancement were well placed. Priesthood and the studies that determined it would come first, however, and no one could tell how one pursuit might affect the other.

December 1696
St. Mark's Cathedral, Venice

We both performed in a Christmas concert at St. Mark's Basilica, the most beautiful cathedral in all of Christendom. I took my position in the fourth row of violinists and felt a nervous excitement in my hands and fingers, waiting in silence until the young *maestro* Antonio Vivaldi would be announced to quiet applause under the curved arches of this glorious Byzantine church. He was a small figure, a proud youngster who always held his back straight and erect to get the most out of the little stature God had granted him. But whenever he stood to play the violin, Antonio was transformed. He was no longer the struggling youth with thin breaths and short legs. When he played, he was an inspired master who brought sighs from the women and beaming smiles from his family.

There were thirty of us present to play that day. We were all boys; in itself, that was a strange twist. There was a conservatory in Venice; well, a school of music, attached to the orphanage. The prefect of the school didn't waste time teaching music to the boys; they were instructed in the trades. The orphan girls were taught music so not having any girls in this concert in St. Mark's might seem a surprise. But to play in the Cathedral – that was reserved for Venice's boys and, mostly, the boys from the families whose brilliance in trade determined the fate of the city.

I pondered all that from the darkened recess near the back of the orchestra as I saw Antonio enter from the left of the altar. His family was not rich or important. But by this tender age he had already achieved a degree of fame that I had long dreamed would be my life's work. It was his mastery of music that placed there on the altar of St. Mark's for this Christmas concert; I thought it a position reserved for families of note in our city. For a moment, I wanted to trade my fine clothing for his second-hand waistcoat.

The nervousness left my hands as I thought about all that. But the feeling that took its place forced an involuntary tightening of my grip on the neck of the violin and bow.

When Antonio entered, he held his violin delicately in one hand, his arm stiff so as not to swing the instrument. In his other hand he held the bow, which he swung carelessly back and forth in rhythm to the little steps he took on the approach. It was as if while protecting the violin he was insouciantly announcing his arrival with the swaying of the bow and smiling at the audience that he already took for his own.

The conductor followed him onto the low step of the altar and then mounted a small platform so that he could be seen by the musicians arranged in rows around him. I heard the clack-clack of his baton as he rapped it on the stand before him, then he raised his arms for a moment and brought both down in one sweep across his chest.

The ten violins in the third and fourth rows began at once, and the sound of a viola chimed in on the second measure. By the fourth measure the woodwinds had joined in and low notes sang from the oboe. The pace of the bowing increased as the composition stretched into its translation section, and I could hear my breathing increase while I focused with intensity on maintaining the pace. The crescendo tipped the sounds of little orchestra into a sudden dive of silence. Although all movement from the musicians had ceased, the last notes hung like an angelic cloud over the audience, echoing softly from the vault of the dome above us.

The conductor held through this pause with his arms raised above his head. After three beats he brought the baton down with such suddenness that it seemed he would lose his balance. But he had coached us in the weeks leading up to this concert to jump into the next measure as soon as his right arm began its downward swing. By the time the baton hit the bottom of the arc, the strings and woodwinds had raised their voices and were praising Almighty God with the all the strength built into them.

Instead of finishing the composition with whispered notes that trailed off into the assembled crowd, the conductor had chosen a piece that ended with a frenzied boom that reverberated off the walls in the interior of St. Mark's long after we had rested our instruments on our knees.

The concert was a great success and it received a sustained applause uncommon in the hallowed space of a cathedral. I was so enthralled with the music and my responsibilities with it that I had no time to study Antonio. But as the sounds of the melody finally drifted away to reside forevermore in the recesses of stone and mosaic that decorated the walls of this church, I noticed him standing in front of the orchestra, bowing to the applause.

When we had completed our work, I carefully wrapped my violin in soft cloth and nestled it into the velvet-lined case that my father had purchased for me. The sacred instrument had appeared on my bed a year ago but only after much discussion and argument.

"What would you do with it?" he asked me repeatedly before giving in to my pleading.

"I will protect it and learn to play it, with mastery," I would reply.

On that afternoon in Christmastide, after packing my violin safely away, I walked from the nave into the crisp air of winter, past people who had cheered the performance but who now hardly noticed me as I emerged from the church. I was an anonymous musician from the unseen rows of other anonymous musicians who lined the back of the orchestra on this night.

I slipped quietly past the gaggle of young girls that surrounded the thin young violinist with blazing red hair. He smiled at his coterie and told small stories, the kind of stories that would come to mind for a self-absorbed young man.

I nodded in Antonio's direction. Was it to be civil and acknowledge his presence, or a feeble attempt to draw some of the attention that surrounded him?

It would have been better if he had ignored my shy plea for attention.

"Domenico!" he said. "Where have you been? I haven't seen you all night."

The stinging comment left me more isolated than I had been sitting in the darkened rows of the minor violinists in the church.

September 1700
Venice

I was celebrating my twenty-first birthday when my father was called to the house of Ludovico d'Invito and his wife, Mariella Costo d'Invito. Signora d'Invito had just given birth to her second child, a girl, whom they named Rachel. I attended my father as he paid his respects to the d'Invito family, a merchant clan of some note but not at the level of our own business, the Trapensi import company. Nevertheless, my father liked Ludovico and – truth be told – conspired to buy his list of clients, so paying tribute to the newborn girl was in order.

We entered the modest d'Invito home and found the signora resting on cushions around the fire. She smiled at us and waved for my father and me to approach. I was tentative, never having been so close to a young baby before, but the light of the mother's smile put me at ease.

There were no servants in this household, unlike my own, so the gathering was by its nature very intimate. With the presence of attendants as we always experienced in the Trapensi family, behavior was a bit stiff so as not to reveal too much of oneself to members outside the family. Over the years, one would develop a veneer that would disguise some of the most intimate intentions. But here, at the d'Invito home, there was no one to intercede between the visitors and the new mother and father. I felt at once uneasy, not knowing how to navigate that scene, but at the same time I felt more at ease because the veneer seemed so superfluous. Especially with the nearness of a young mother exposing her breast to nurse the infant girl.

The light of the fireplace cast dancing shadows on the scene and yet I could see how beautiful the young baby's face was – Rachel as I was introduced to her at that moment – and how the force of an mother's love could fill the room.

My father paid his respects to Ludovico, which included a small sack of money – the more commonplace demonstration of congratulations among merchants – and then he begged his leave. He was at the door with his hat already on his head but I was still at the mother's side, smiling back at the baby Rachel who looked deeply into my eyes.

Suddenly, a crackle from the fire and a burst of unexpected flame from the embers startled both me and Signora d'Invito. The baby was also startled, and gave a brief cry of surprise, but then settled back into her mother's clutch and closed her eyes.

"We should go," my father said, noticing the scene and perhaps wondering why his son was so absorbed with the infant.

"Yes, sir," I replied while still staring at the baby. "We should leave them to rest."

I raised my hat to Signora d'Invito that I held respectfully in my right hand, then settled it on my head in a signal that I would depart.

"Thank you for coming," she said quietly. "I will remember your kindness."

My father and I left the d'Invito home that afternoon but I could not forget the impression that was made upon me of a woman just birthing, and a baby so new and so beautiful.

September 1703
Venice

By the early months of summer, my father began talking to me more seriously about the Trapensi shipping business. He described my music studies as a 'dalliance' that 'a future son of business could ill afford.'

I was an obedient son and nodded assent to his decrees. It's true that I harbored a lingering desire to be recognized as a great violinist, but I was now twenty-five and no such accolades were coming my way. I returned to my violin in the velvet-lined case now and then, but less frequently in recent years and, at some point, abandoned it altogether.

My father smiled thankfully at me as he noticed the change in my demeanor. I would be his successor and, although he was not yet old, he wanted me to enter the business full time so that he could be assured that I would know all there was about the enterprise before death claimed him.

I seldom saw Antonio in recent years. As I receded from the music scene, he became more involved in it. I heard some comments about him, some regarding his music but some because his father had delved deeper into the world of music too. Stories were circulating that the barber could barely feed his large family on his normal proceeds and music offered an alternative form of income. I knew that was only partly true. I compared Giovanni and Antonio to my father and me and knew that Antonio was not only blessed with musical brilliance but with a father who recognized it and fostered it in the young man in his household.

Of course, I didn't blame my father. I told myself that he too recognized brilliance where it could be found, but he found no such musical talent in our family and so he pushed me toward a career for which I seemed better suited.

As a member of the merchant class, I received the customary invitation to attend the annual Christmas concert at St. Mark's. Once or twice I went, but in time I decided that my attendance wasn't needed at the festivities.

Antonio had finally been ordained into the priesthood in the spring of this year. It was never clear to me why he took ten years to complete the training. I doubted that it was because of a lack of intelligence. Instead, I concluded – as I'm sure his father did – that Antonio was just insufficiently interested in the teachings of the Church. In Venice, to be ordained was a sign of accomplishment, but it was also taken as a sign that the young man in question had taken a road that promised a secure future, whether he was devoted to the matters of God or not. Antonio was sent to his studies by his father and he accepted the role, but he never seemed to be right for the position.

In the meantime, I was apprenticed to my father and preparing to shoulder the full set of responsibilities of running the import business. Antonio continued to move between his roles as young cleric and accomplished composer, devoting some of his spare time to theological studies but most of it to playing his violin and scratching notes down on bits of paper that he would later turn into his compositions and lead to performances before admiring crowds.

The bishop noticed the slow progress that Antonio had made but cheered the ultimate success of donning the cloth. Still, rumors had it that he expected little of the musician turned cleric. Antonio celebrated mass on two occasions over the next few months, far fewer than what is normally expected of new celebrants. Further complicating his low level of desire for the priesthood, he complained of shortness of breath – the malady that had afflicted him since birth. After standing at the altar and loudly proclaiming the words of God, he would sometimes be reduced to coughing and wheezing. And he began to complain that standing for long periods on the altar left him exhausted after each service.

The bishop regarded that plea as half true. He knew that Antonio suffered from constricted breathing, but he hadn't noticed any reluctance on the musician's part to stand for long stretches of time with his violin under his chin.

* * *

After about six months serving his duties as a part-time priest, Antonio was awarded a position as a *maestro di violino* at the *Conservatorio dell'Ospedale della Pietà.* The hospital itself – the *Ospedale* – was one of four in Venice that tended to the orphaned and abandoned children. This one treated the girls and boys separately and prepared them for their future. The boys were instructed in the trades, mostly the lower order of manual workers like carpenters and dockhands. The girls were introduced to music and encouraged to develop whatever skills they had to lighten the burden of daily toil for their future husbands.

For this training, the girls spent their time at the *Conservatorio* which was managed as part of the hospital but with a distinctly separate curriculum. The music teachers were often men which meant that these young girls spent their days under the control and constant supervision of older men.

Antonio was employed in just such a position. He was, by the time of his appointment to the *Conservatorio*, only twenty-five years old, so considerably younger than the paunchy gray-haired men on the staff. The girls that were assigned to Antonio's instruction were all under the age of eighteen, some of them as young as eleven years old. Those from ten years of age and younger were not considered ready to be taught the intricacies of music or the proper behavior for girls on the verge of womanhood. Their instruction was focused on the courtesies of civilized life in Venice and in beginning lessons in sewing and cooking.

My father was a benefactor of *L'Ospedale della Pietà* and he promised that the Trapensi family would actively provide funds for the care and training of the young girls. The entire establishment was mostly supported by the Republic of Venice, but the government leaders appreciated contributions from successful businessmen. The generosity of these donors was noticed by the city fathers, who sustained the generosity of these wealthy families by the grant of special privileges in Venice. It was through my father's involvement that I became a regular visitor to the hospital, usually as the one assigned to bring our periodic contributions to the rector at the institution and to tour the facility to prove that our money was being wisely spent.

Upon arrival, I was routinely directed to the wing reserved for the boys and, while there, was allowed to tour the trade laboratories with all the latest tools and equipment. Certain boys, those with practiced skill, would be called over to demonstrate the operation of the lathe, or the assembly of plates of brass letters used in the printing press, or the molds used for glass blowing that had recently been brought to Venice by the artisans in Murano. These tours often took a few hours, and I was ushered out to the courtyard of the school after seeing the boys at work.

On occasion, I was allowed to sit in on a practice session of the girls playing their instruments. These were not organized affairs; certainly not concerts. The large room allowed some space for each of the girls to work their instruments – from violins and violas to clarinets and flutes – but produced a cacophony of unrelated sounds that made the audible experience of the room hard to take for very long. Despite the apparent disorganization of the practice, all of the girls were expected to outfit themselves in clean dresses of the appropriate length, and to wear their hair tied back in a ribboned bow. The visual effect of beauty, however, was insufficient to overcome the audible effect of disorder.

The male teachers, mostly men older than I was, walked among the girls offering suggestions and reprimands, and coaching the young students to pluck or bow or breathe in the prescribed way.

On more than one of these visits to the *Conservatorio,* I encountered Antonio. His genius at music put him in a position to teach at his young age, far earlier than the other teachers, and with his small stature and youthful looks, he at times appeared to a member of the class, not the instructor. Except that he was a man, not a girl.

On a few of these trips to the *Conservatorio,* I entered just as Antonio was about to begin his session with his female orchestra.

"Hello, my friend," he said as I entered the room full of young girls. "It is good to see you. Have you come for a violin lesson?"

The comment stung my pride, much like the comment that he had made outside St. Mark's at the Christmas concert several years back. Without being overtly offensive, Antonio found it easy to belittle me in public, and this added to my growing disdain for the man. To have him do this in front of a roomful of young girls made it even worse for me. I blushed because I couldn't come up with a quick reply, but my tormentor saved me. Turning to the assembled girls, he continued.

"This is my good friend Domenico Trapensi. He, too, is an accomplished musician, but his greatest skill resides in business."

He turned his eyes back toward me but continued in a voice loud enough for the girls to hear over his shoulder.

"He will inherit his father's import business and do well and proper by it." Then turning back toward his class, he concluded, "And I think his family's legacy will be the greater for it."

The blood subsided from my cheeks and I was able to bring a little smile to my face. Antonio's ability to embarrass me and then praise me in the same breath was frightening, but I knew him well and I knew that his mastery of the violin could sometimes be matched by his mastery of words.

Antonio thrived in that environment. He all but abandoned his priestly duties; instead he spent his days in front of the class of adoring girls – girls who seemed to smile too broadly and fuss with their hair to readily whenever he entered the room. Of course, as a priest, he hadn't married, so he spent his nights alone in his apartment composing music.

Or, at least, I heard that he was alone. I was not in his circle anymore and I didn't have a social relationship with him. There were rumors that the all-female ensemble was too great a temptation for a young man like Antonio, and that he occasionally took advantage of the romantic whims of the girls in the evening hours when he was said to be writing his music.

My life was different. I too was not yet married but I was spending more time than ever in my father's business. As he receded from the routine duties of the business, he seemed to release his hold on his health, as if the time had come not only to rest, but to fall into a state of inactivity. As he had hinted in bringing me further into the Trapensi business, I began to assume that he would follow my mother in death in a short time, when the full responsibility for the import house would fall to me.

July 1704
Venice

"It's time," Dario shouted to me.

He was my father's dock manager, a burly man who managed the ships that arrived in clockwork fashion. Dario was standing in his usual position on the harbor, perched upon the last planks of the wooden dock that jutted out into the canal. His left foot was raised and placed upon a bale of textiles tied together in a knot; his right foot was anchored on the dock itself. He waved his arm at me as if to point out the arrival of another ship, one of the Trapensi fleet of supply vessels bringing prized goods to our home port in Venice.

I raised my chin and looked toward Dario's arm pointing outward toward the broad sea beyond our port. In the distance I could make out the faint silhouette of sails above a dark wooden hulk gliding across the waters in the Venetian Lagoon. How Dario knew that it was one of my father's shippers I couldn't imagine. But I watched it approach and, after a few more hours, it finally docked at the Trapensi loading platform.

Dario was right, as always – my father was rich enough that he only hired the best. The captain of the ship could be heard calling for his crew to raise and bind the sails and furl them at the cross-beams. Other sailors hustled across the deck and threw lines to Dario's men on the shore. Together, they roped the great vessel to the dock and gently pulled it toward its berth.

When the ship was bound to the shore, a quiet settled over everyone. The task of bringing the vessel home was completed and much work remained in unloading the cargo, but for now, the sailors would eat – and drink – and attention would shift to the ac-countants and registrars. They disembarked first to meet with Dario, who escorted them to the counting house. There, over a long meal and much wine, they provided details on what the ship carried, counted items lost and gained, and conducted a tally of the value of the shipment. They were the second level merchants, learned accountants who knew banking and commerce but had not secured investment cap-ital for themselves yet. Anyone with an eye could see that they intended to raise the funds to make a shipping business of their own.

After all, this was Venice, the greatest import city in the world.

The table was set with platters of fattened meat, larded endive and onion, and bottomless jugs of red wine. Conversation was quiet and polite at first but it became looser and more gregarious with consumption of the vinous blood. The room was two floors above the dock and a wide window opened onto the ships below and showcased the bustling port of Venice. The air at this time of year was easy, the breeze light, and the guests enjoyed being entertained at such a prime spot in the city.

I joined Dario and the others for the meal, although I remained quiet throughout. My chair was set at the head of the table as my father's representative, but I did not need to participate in the exchange economy that was taking place at the seats around me. I listened carefully to Dario's speech, however, mindful that he was the first line representative who determined the profit and losses not only for my father's business, but for my future.

"Signor Trapensi," he said to me near the end of the meal. "Do you agree with these prices?"

It was a rhetorical question. I did not have Dario's acumen in such things, but he needed my consent to complete the deal.

"*Si*," I replied, to which Dario smiled and nodded.

I was the first born in the family. My mother had failed in three later pregnancies and then died in childbirth fourteen years ago, along with the child, so I was left with no siblings. I was Domenico Trapensi to my friends and my father but to Dario and the others, I was Signor Trapensi, the only son of an ambitious shipper who had surpassed his con-temporaries and owned the most successful import house in Venice. From this city, we could control the price of fine silk, sugar cane, and exquisite jewelry from the East, along with many other staples of civ-ilized society.

Dario knew this, which was why he served as an ingratiating servant to my father. He also knew – disguised perhaps in his obsequious performance – that his role might not be the same when my fa-ther passed the business on to me, so his smiles and bows sometimes came across as too flattering for the point he was trying to make.

* * *

While Dario conducted the business of my family, I reached for the cup of wine that the servant has just dutifully refilled. As my mind drew a curtain across the reality of the men assembled at the table, the conversation seemed to me to drop to an unconscious whisper. The boat's captain and mate still addressed Dario and he replied, but they seemed to be talking in another room. My thoughts drifted back toward my youthful days of music, and I all but lost track of the momentous decisions being made at the table. Even their occasional outbursts of laughter seemed muffled, as if in a dream.

I lifted the cup of wine and as my elbow bent to bring it to my lips, I imagined that I was raising a violin to my chin. The delightful flavors cascading down my throat were no longer wine, but the imagined strains of musical notes as they entered my senses. My imagination took me back to the quiet moments spent in the sunlight of the afternoon, standing just inside the window of my room, with the violin nestled beneath my chin and the bow poised over the neck of the instrument.

The sound of men's conversation returned to me, almost as if they themselves were returning to the room, and so too did my thoughts resolve into the present. I stood from the table and moved over to gaze out the broad window overlooking the docks as the long meal ended.

Dario shook the hands of slapped the backs of the agents from the ship. He had concluded the trade and was folding his ledger to return to the counting house at the Trapensi offices, and the other men were departing through the door. No one stopped to shake my hand or offer their goodbyes. I was just the owner of the business; Dario was the man they had to deal with.

But he approached me at the window when the room had emptied.

"It is good, Signor Trapensi," he said. "It has been a good day."

Dario didn't slap my back as he did with the others; physical contact between agents and owners was not the custom. But he did look into my eyes, a gesture that some would interpret as inappropriate but which I knew to be a signal from this man in my employ. He knew the business better than I did, and he wanted me to remember that I needed him. More importantly, he wanted me to remember to treat him with deference if I wanted the business to continue.

When Dario left the room, I stayed at the window. There were huge ships, dockhands moving about, and great cranes to lift the cargo from the gently rocking decks of the vessels and deliver the boxes and bales to the wagons waiting on the pier. The azure skies formed a heavenly dome over the scene, and the lapping of the green waves tapped out the rhythm of the activity below. I was a privileged member of the moneyed class in the greatest city in the world. But I didn't know where my life would lead, or how I would find my way in it.

* * *

Antonio's activities in the priestly custom continued to decline. After excusing himself in consecutive weeks from the performance of the sacraments, he was called in to speak with the bishop. The meeting took place on a day that I was visiting *L'Ospedale* and I saw him going down the long portico that surrounded the building. He made eye contact with me and offered a little smile but passed by with little more.

When I had completed my tour of the boys' laboratories, I encountered Antonio once again.

"Hello, Domenico," he said in a flat tone of voice. It seemed that the audience with the bishop had left him dispirited.

"Hello, Antonio," I replied, but continued, "And how are you today?" Certainly, such a direct query would reveal something about his encounter with the prelate.

"Quite well, actually," he said, but then he coughed.

"Just a bit of a wheeze," he explained, tapping his throat lightly with his finger.

* * *

I found out more on my exit from the building. Antonio had been given a dispensation from saying mass because of his health, but at the same time he was saddled with additional duties in music composition and instruction. It seemed odd to me that the liturgical duties could be so tiring but that he could still manage the weight of music classes.

In fact, I also found out that Antonio had received additional duties at the same time. I do not know whether these new assignments were intended to make up for time now freed from liturgical duties, but it is doubtful. The bishop gave Antonio the dispensation from saying mass, but the new duties – all musical – were assigned by the director of the *Conservatorio.*

Commencing immediately, Antonio would begin work as the *viola all'inglese,* a performer's role that wouldn't require that he instruct others but that he must appear in – and sometimes orchestrate – compositions that included this instrument.

September 1705
Piazza San Marco, Venice

Antonio walked through the crowds of the Piazza San Marco today, carving a path through the throngs while somehow managing to hollow out a bubble of space around himself. He smiled and waved his right hand, but I couldn't quite interpret his meaning. Was it a signal of greeting to the throngs or just his manner of clearing a path for himself and his retinue? Young girls were bunched behind him – indulgent students from his music class, no doubt – and they were followed closely by a gaggle of younger children whose clothing bespoke of the modest incomes. Last behind these was a ragtag army of adolescents who followed every celebrity, known or unrecognized, who strode across the stones in this great piazza.

I recognized some of the children in the second group, those with the means to afford decent clothing. There was Brie d'Invito, a seven-year old who was already apprenticed to a tradesman known to my father. Brie would be learning a manual trade, not one of business such as the Trapensi enterprise, but his skill would no doubt continue the modest success of the d'Invito family.

With Brie was his younger sister Rachel who had just turned five earlier this year. I had visited the d'Invito family with my father at the child's birth, and the circumstances of our business relationship assured that I, as the representative of the wealthy Trapensi family, would be included in the six-month public announcement of Rachel's birth. It was customary for families to wait this amount of time before publicly proclaiming the birth since so many babies did not survive the challenges of early life.

In proper measure, I called on the family just after the announcement to pay my respects and offer the Trapensi gift to the parents. It was a silver bowl with the family name engraved upon it. When I presented it to the child's mother, she smiled broadly and asked if I would want to see the baby. At first, I declined. I had never had much luck with infants, having no siblings to teach me how, and I feared that being near this one might bring bad luck to one of us.

But the radiant mother pressed me forward to a crib festooned with lacy ribbons. When she reached her hand up to part the gossamer drapes, I looked down upon the most beautiful baby that I had ever seen. Well, so I thought to myself; in fact I had seen very few babies but this one must still be the most beautiful ever born. I smiled despite myself and cocked my head at an angle. Baby Rachel smiled back and let out a little squeal that frightened me at first, but her mother was ecstatic.

"No, this is wonderful. Rachel is a very happy baby, and she is showing you that she is happy to meet you."

I doubted that so much could be teased out of that little yelp, but I still enjoyed her mother's recitation of it.

That was five years ago and as I stood there in Piazza San Marco and Rachel skipped past, I smiled once more at the lovely little thing. She was beautiful as a baby and even more so now that her light blond hair was so full and curly, and tumbling down to her shoulders.

Later in the evening, Maestro Vivaldi put on a performance for the church elders and the congregation. It was conducted in the Basilica at the conclusion of the sacred mass, a tribute to great music that was sure to keep the faithful in the pews beyond the benediction at the end of the services. It was a sweet and, at times, heroic performance, a composition that alternated between the whisper of angels' voices and the explosive throbbing of a heart in ecstasy. My attention, and that of the other adults in the church, was riveted on him. It was as if the violinists sitting in support behind the maestro had faded into oblivion and only Vivaldi himself shone in the single ray of sunlight that penetrated the darkness of the Basilica.

Another thing that I noticed was that the composition was intense and seductive, with notes that were at once innocently romantic as well as suggestive of roguish intent. It almost seemed inappropriate to be played in the nave of a consecrated church; and it was a good thing no younger children were present to hear the music and, perhaps, be indulged by it.

But this was no secret in Vivaldi's portfolio of music that he was assembling. For a man with weak lungs, he was amazingly expressive when it came to his musical compositions. I sat with him on several occasions and listened how he described the sonnets he wrote to accompany the music, lyrics to make plain the images that he was conjuring with his melodies.

"That is not necessary," I told him. "I know everything you intend before I even read the words that you've scribbled down."

That pleased Antonio, but not enough to convince him to overcome his obsession with perfection.

"The words are there to remind me," he said, as if I believed that this genius needed scribbled notes to resurrect the mental images he portrayed so clearly in his music.

"Just so," I countered, "but you don't sing the music, you only play it. How is anyone to know what you've written any way other than my way...to hear and translate the sounds into sights?"

"Okay," Antonio rejoined, then, "I will write something with lyrics...if I think the music requires it!"

* * *

It was also in this year of Seventeen Hundred and Five that the first notebook of Antonio's compositions was published. I knew that it was only a matter of time; the soaring notes and intricate melodies that captivated audiences when he played them could be replicated by other musicians – lesser human beings, no doubt – and the world would grow in its appreciation for the music that Antonio could conjure up.

Many of the pieces were duets for violin. He was such a gifted composer and performer himself that I was surprised at first to discover that he would share the stage with another violinist. But then I recalled a recent visit to the *Conservatorio* when I happened to be walking past his studio. Antonio was playing something that I had not heard before and a young woman was sitting beside him, also with a violin under her chin. She managed to concentrate on her music as much as she focused on her teacher at that moment, while Antonio played with his eyes closed and his mind completely absorbed with the music.

His partner in this duet was one of the older girls, with the blonde hair of a northern Italian and the mature figure of womanhood. But Antonio didn't notice that, and he didn't notice the attention that she paid to him.

I watched closely from just outside the door until they had completed the composition, then swung around behind the doorframe when Antonio's eyes opened.

"You are coming along very well," I heard him say to his pupil. "I have no doubt that you will become a fine musician one day."

As he paid her these compliments, I imagined that I was the one sitting on the small chair beside her, and that I was the one offering such praise to this attractive young lady.

As I walked down the rest of the corridor, I replayed parts of the duet in my head but could not say with certainty that I had heard it before. Knowing that Antonio was under a contract to compile new musical pieces for publication, I assumed that this was the result of that effort. Little did I know at the time but that this piece would be gathered with other Vivaldi productions and soon published by Giuseppe Sala, a well-known printer in Venice who had arranged the contract with the *maestro*.

Sala had become well acquainted of Antonio's work. And yet, initially, despite his bias toward the musician, he had to be convinced that publication of a slate of works by Vivaldi would make financial sense, so he talked Antonio into a rigorous production schedule that include twelve compositions. Taken together, the notebook was named Opus 1 and it was published very soon after the ink had dried on Antonio's last musical score.

True to the careful planning of the printer, the notebook sold very well and made a good profit for Sala and Vivaldi. And in the process, Antonio's reputation took another step up.

I was one of the buyers of that notebook. For all the times that I had listened from a distance when Antonio played his violin, I could not copy his performance. But once I had the score in my hands, I could hardly wait to try it myself.

I quickly scanned the contents looking for a duet that seemed to represent what I had heard from Antonio and the young lady on that recent afternoon. When I found it, my first thought was to play his part and imagine his partner to be there in the room with me. But although Antonio's role was more central to the theme of the composition, it was clear that this work would sound hollow without another violin filling in the gaps.

Instead I chose another concerto that had been written for a soloist and I prepared myself to play it.

My father was in the house when I retrieved the long-unused violin from the closet at the back of my bed chamber. The strings were still in satisfactory condition, but not very pliable. I had to tune the instrument carefully, fearful that putting too much pressure in twisting the tuning knobs on the peg-box might well rip the twisted gut strings in half. I applied gentle pressure to each of the four strings until I believed I had brought the instrument into acceptable shape. Once there, I drew the bow across the upper strings, then the lower, and slowed my breathing as I had been taught so many years before.

The notes that lifted from the violin pleased me and I smiled. I had no illusions about my expertise, but to be able to produce the sounds of the violin again after so many years was soothing for my heart and my spirit.

Satisfied that all was in order, I placed my copy of Antonio's notebook on the stand at the piano. When I gave up the violin some years before, the music stand disappeared too, so that now I had to use the piano's stand for the same purpose and lean over the piano bench to see the notes clearly.

My first efforts were poorly executed, a fact that was painfully obvious to me and possibly also to the violin itself. But I tried again and, with patience and concentration, was able to bear down on the strings with the right pressure to produce the proper notes.

A halting melody emerged from my persistence. The tone of the notes was not completely whole, the rhythm was off, and the angel's breath that can be heard in each note of a master's violin was missing. But I was thrilled at being able to play the composition through to its conclusion.

When I finished and dropped my bow hand to my side, I noticed my father standing in the doorway. He did not speak and had no real expression on his face. But once noticed, he turned a scolding look my way, then spun on his heel and disappeared down the stone hallway that led to his own room.

I looked at the score again but I no longer had the energy or mood to attempt it. I tapped the bow on the piano bench a few times, almost in deep contemplation of what to do next, then I raised my chin from the lower body of the violin and let my left arm and the violin drop to my side.

With a sigh, I closed Antonio's notebook and returned my instrument to its case, then returned the case to its corner in my closet.

October 1707
Venice

"It shouldn't be so difficult," I heard as I walked past the girls' music room. I was on another inspection of *L'Ospedale* and found myself once more drawn to the place where the girls were being trained.

The voice was that of Antonio; I knew it well. Although the comment seemed critical, I detected a lilting note of sarcasm in it, even before I turned toward my right and slipped in through the open doorway.

Antonio was standing behind one of the older girls, wrapping his arms around her, and he held his hands over hers on the violin, one holding the neck of the instrument; the other gripping the bow lightly between her fingers. Antonio's arms were not long and his position forced him to stand very close to the girl from behind. To reach the same position as her hands required a close embrace that drew the blood into the cheeks of the girl herself.

Even some of the girls in the room who should have been concentrating on their own techniques had paused to watch; some of them were whispering comments to their seatmates and giggling.

"It shouldn't be so difficult," he repeated, lifting his right hand with hers to slide the bow forward across the strings, then pulling it back, and then forward again. It seemed to me that the girl was not even trying, but simply standing in the circle of Antonio's arms and enjoying the close contact without any effort put forward to play the instrument.

After a moment, I realized that my own cheeks were hot, so I turned quickly to exit through the door that I had entered.

* * *

On that same afternoon, I was crossing a bridge that led to the *Chiesa di San Beneto* and encountered Antonio. He was not heading in the direction of his apartment but was accompanied by a young lady whom I did not immediately recognize. She seemed careful to remain anonymous, as she had pulled her hood farther over her head and down across the auburn hair that curled out into view. As they passed by me, Antonio nodded in a friendly way and I returned the gesture.

Even in this close contact, I could not recognize the woman.

That evening, after having my fill of supper, I grew restless and wanted the contact of other human beings. My father remained in our home nearly every day since my mother passed away, but his temperament was suited to the cold climes of a stone building. I was a young man who still fancied the company of men and women and sought the comforts of such a society in the cafés and *ristoranti* of the day.

After the autumn sun had retired for the evening, I went down to the street and steered quite unconsciously toward Piazza San Marco. There would be fun and music, and wine and beer, and so that would be the place for me to find entertainment.

At Café Ridolfo, I found a table that offered a view of the piazza itself, better yet since the perch was two steps above the cobblestones and the collected hoard of people meandered below me as if I was on a dais. Ferdinando, the waiter who had tended to me on another night, arrived quickly and promised a bottle of the red wine from Veneto, the wine that he remembered that I preferred. With a thankful wave of my hand, I sent Ferdinando on his errand and turned my attention back to the square.

There were several rows of little tables and chairs on the pavement below me, additional seating to accommodate the many customers that Café Ridolfo always attracted. These tables were nearly filled also, just as those on the portico where I sat were nearly filled, and the chatter from twos and threes and fours who occupied the chairs created a delightful if cacophonous symphony for my ears.

Beyond the outer row of tables there were men selling flowers and sweet treats. There were dogs wandering about the throng looking for scraps that had fallen from the tables, and the ubiquitous pigeons that flocked to the square to the delight of children, and to the chagrin of the adults.

Wandering musicians strummed fat guitars and blew on wooden horns to perform for the crowd and collect some loose change. Some approached couples seated at the tables and begged for the opportunity to perform a private serenade – for a small donation, of course. And there were the women with opulent breasts proudly displayed above the lace of their bodice in search of a very different type of customer.

I observed all this humanity and smiled at the folly of it all. These were people in search of happiness and pleasure. Some would find it tonight, though mostly a fleeting version of it. Others would drink until little opportunity remained and then they would return to their simple homes to sleep off the wine and wait for another day.

I had the great good luck of being born into the Trapensi family, luck which promised that I would live above the means of these people and enjoy happiness and pleasure the likes of which they would never know.

A controlled laugh arose from someone on my right so I twisted around in my chair to peer beyond the stone column that separated my table from the others. I saw a clutch of chairs surrounding another table on the same level as mine, set close in to the edge of the portico and sandwiched between the third and fourth columns. The voice of one woman, then another, and then the soft voice of a man reached me.

I leaned farther back in my chair but tried to remain unobtrusive in doing so. There was a table of three women and a man. The ladies all appeared to be just less than my age, but not too young, and then I realized from his voice that the man was Vivaldi. I looked again and listened like a voyeur to their conversation. The women laughed as they spoke, covering their mouths to hide their smiles, yet each dared to touch Antonio's arm as they addressed him. Such a display of public intimacy would not even be dared by a married couple. And it was all three of the women who expressed themselves in this way.

One of the ladies turned my way and I quickly looked down, embarrassed that I had been caught staring. It was then that I saw her shoes. They were a bright green with golden buttons on them. And just as I realized this, my subconscious drew up the image of the feet of the woman that Antonio had accompanied across the bridge that afternoon. She wore bright green shoes with gold buttons.

I couldn't resist and so raised my eyes to look upon the woman wearing the green shoes. She sat facing me slightly from the side and smiling at me as if she then knew what I had discovered. Her hair was auburn, parted down the middle and braided from the crown of her head in the manner of many of the wealthy women of the time. She nodded briefly but then turned her attention back to her female friends and to Antonio.

Once I had seen her face, I recognized her. She was the Lady Adelfio, married to Luigi Adelfio, a successful merchant who dealt frequently with the Trapensi house. I wondered why she didn't show any embarrassment at being in the company of another man, why she didn't show any concern that her presence here would raise talk and suspicions. But while my thoughts ran to rumor and ruin, she turned her attention back to laughter and pleasure.

* * *

Antonio's reputation was rewarded with further income not only from *L'Ospedale* but also from the performances that he was called upon more often to deliver. As a result of his improved status, he was able to rent an apartment near the Piazza San Marco, into which his entire family moved. With so many siblings, this might have been a crowded environment, but he made more money than his father – more money than many Venetians – and he could afford a place that was large enough for everyone.

I saw him one day as he was about to board a gondola. His home was behind the piazza, not across the canal, so he wasn't headed home.

"Where are you going?" I called out, more as the simple, polite conversation of an acquaintance than as an actual interest in his affairs.

"I have a meeting at the *Basilica di Santa Maria della Salute*," he said. It was a church across the main canal of Venice, an edifice that soared toward the heavens at nearly the height of its more famous neighbor, *Basilica San Marco*. It was built in prayer to the Holy Mary who rescued us from the plague.

"What is there?" I asked. It was an impertinent question, but I had now come to the conclusion that not all of Antonio's intentions were noble and I wanted to entertain myself with his stories.

"A student," was all he said, as he waved goodbye.

May 1708
Venice

I hadn't seen Antonio for some months but knew that his success had resulted in more trips abroad. He performed in the various towns in Veneto but also in other places such as Roma and as far away as Milano. I assumed that he had multiple reasons for doing so. Certainly, the money was good and as he enjoyed the fine life he became even more interested in establishing his career. However, I also had heard that he was looking for a wealthy sponsor, someone whose position could be enjoyed by Antonio and who could give him access to the houses of royalty throughout Europe.

Such endless trips made in a drafty carriage across bumpy and over sometimes flooded roads was exactly the kind of effort shunned by my father.

"Those who have established themselves," he always said, "should not have to travel. The world should come to them."

And yet, I often thought of venturing outside of Venice just as my itinerant friend did. The small villages of the countryside and the big cities dotting

the land could become a collection of memories use-
ful in moments of quiet and solitude in the Trapensi
merchant house. Even my agent, Dario, had traveled extensively, although he counted foreign ports
of business among his explorations. I did not share
my father's contempt for travel, yet, still, I didn't
expect to experience much myself.

The news of the world came to our port daily, a
commodity that could not be sold but which might
carry value equal to that of the textiles and wheat
brought in on a regular basis. It was a warm summer
day that I greeted Filipe du Mont, a friend of our
family and the representative of his own merchan-
dising business. His specialty was gold and silver,
which he delivered to the jewelers and craftsmen of
our city to turn into the glittering ornaments that
decorated the wealthy ladies of Venice.

"He is an amazing fellow," he said as he bounded
down the gangway.

"Who?" I asked.

"That friend of yours, Vivaldi!"

He normally traveled by sea, as he had just done,
and so I couldn't imagine where he had encountered
Antonio.

"Where did you see him?" I winced at even replying to his question, since my query would suggest some interest in the musician.

"He was in Rovigo a fortnight ago. Gave a marvelous performance. But you wouldn't believe it -- he had a woman singing the music that he performed at her side."

I was certain that Filipe was mistaken. Antonio the maestro composed instrumental music, nearly all for violin, and much designed for his own instrument.

"I don't think he was in Rovigo, Filipe. Besides, he doesn't compose music for vocals."

"He did this time," Filipe replied, taking me by the arm and guiding us along the quay toward the *Piazza San Marco*. I knew the café that he liked and I knew that this was the direction in which we were heading. It was the middle of the day and since most of the Venetian men were occupied with their trades and their wives with their children, there was a smaller than usual crowd as we walked toward Café Bostrom.

"He played his usual fine music," Filipe said, as he raised his free hand and swept it in a grand motion that took in the entire sky. "And she was fantastic.

Beautiful voice," and then he lowered his voice to a whisper, "but that wasn't what I noticed at first."

Filipe pulled us toward Café Bostrom as he described the woman's shape and the color of her hair, taking a moment to describe her gown in more detail than I would have expected from a man who pedaled gold and jewels.

"She was young, but a bit older than your friend, and she seemed very much in love with the music."

"And by that," I began, "do you mean not very much in love with the musician?"

Filipe laughed, since he knew Antonio's reputation. I quickly thought back to the stories that I, myself, had told of the *maestro's* character, trying to determine whether any had been told by me with a note of jealousy.

"Oh, no," he replied, sitting down lightly at a table outside the café. "She didn't even seem to notice him."

I considered that thought and wondered whether Antonio had auditioned girls for his vocal composition with more interest in their voices than other attributes.

"So, as I have told you, your friend is an amazing fellow."

This news took a few moments for me to process, which I did while we waited for the waiter to appear. Antonio was certainly more interested in his music, although I had heard too many stories and witnessed too many incidents involving him and young girls to dismiss the rumors. But, as Filipe had said, perhaps his newly composed vocals required a careful distance between him and the woman drawn in to perform her role.

After the waiter arrived to take our order, Filipe retrieved a folded program from his coat pocket and handed it to me. It was a program announcement with Antonio Vivaldi's name at the top in the largest print, below which was Giuseppina Canciole, noted as a singer from Rovigo who would perform with the visiting violinist. Just below her name in a print that was larger than hers and yet smaller than Antonio's was the name of the featured piece, *Le Gare del Dovere.* The program announced that a concert would be performed on that evening and would be highlighted by a new composition written by the famous composer, "the first to be written for vocalization."

"It was *bellissima*," Filipe added, as if he had not yet already communicated his approval of the work.

"And the woman!" he added with excitement. Antonio certainly knows how to choose his partners."

From Filipe's raised eyebrows and dancing smile, I couldn't tell whether Antonio had chosen this Giuseppina as his partner in music or love. Or both. Or whether, in fact, Filipe knew anything about it.

* * *

Filipe and I passed a pleasant afternoon at the café and when I rose to return to the merchant house, he said that he had someone that he wanted to visit. It was a woman, which was obvious from the way he said it, and I envied him all the more. He was married to an intelligent and beautiful woman in Marseilles and seemed to keep others in the various ports that he visited. I was thirty years old and unmarried, and seemed to lack even the vacuous romances that my friend enjoyed in the cities that dotted his travel circuit.

After he left, I began my walk across the piazza and down the quay to return to the Trapensi business office. Lost in thought, I nearly passed by Signora d'Invito who was walking her young daughter, Rachel, in the opposite direction. The girl was now eight years old and had already become a fetching young girl. Not a woman in the sense of maturity, but her rosy cheeks and silky hair bore great promise for the future.

"*Buon giorno*," I offered, tipping my hat to the signora.

"*Buon giorno*," she replied, and then leaned slightly down to her daughter and said, "Rachel, this is Signor Trapensi, a very important man in Venice."

Rachel said nothing but offered a tiny smile and a curtsy as well-groomed girls were taught to do.

"How are you, my little one?" I said to her.

Rachel's mother paused for a moment while she waited for the girl to choose to respond. Then her daughter fulfilled the promise of good breeding.

"I am well, kind sir," but then nothing more.

I tipped my hat again and continued on my way, pleased at having the opportunity to see the striking Signora d'Invito and her pretty daughter.

* * *

When I reached the office, my father stood with Dario at the large table in the room. They were focused on papers spread out before them and exchanged questions and answers concerning the contents.

"*Buona sera*," my father said, and I inferred from his 'good evening' that he considered my arrival to be too late in the day.

"*Buon giorno*, father," I replied, not willing to give him that opening. Dario stood by quietly, his hands resting on the table as his body leaned over it.

"We will have cotton arriving from the south, and some silks from the east," my father informed me. "They come tomorrow, both ships, just before midday."

He didn't have to give me instructions or detail what my responsibilities were. He was merely reminding me without specifics that he had turned over control of the Trapensi business to me and that I must be more prepared. Dario looked on – was that a little look of amusement on his face? – but didn't say anything.

"Of course. I will be here," I replied, "just as I always am."

It was true that I was not in the house as often or for as long as my father was; he seldom left the Trapensi house anymore. But I did not intend to live the life of a widower before I was even married!

My father nodded and left the room. Dario stood up straight at the patriarch's departure, and then looked at me.

"He misses your mother," he said, "and worries about your future."

I understood what Dario was saying, but I didn't need to be reminded of it by my employee.

September 1709
Venice

"And why so glum?" I asked Antonio when I encountered him at the Café Ridolfo, at his usual table but not in his usual mood. His right hand was wrapped around the short tumbler filled with red wine, his chin rested near his chest, and his eyes stared blankly at the bloody liquid in the glass. He didn't reply at once, so I sat down at the table with him, my back to the piazza which he faced.

I admit that I was a bit cheered by his glum expression and I had to overcome my own good feelings in order to continue the conversation.

"What is it, Antonio?" Do you have bad news about your music? Or your situation at the *Conservatorio?*" I paused then but couldn't resist. "Or does it have to do with a woman?" I knew that he had developed a reputation as a lady's man, although I was unsure whether that reputation was simply concocted out of other men's fantasies, because I actually had seen Antonio with a woman very few times, and at that only in unclear circumstances.

He remained quiet for a moment longer, then took a draft of the wine and set the glass down a bit too rudely.

"No," he said, sitting up straighter and putting a smile on his face. "It's the teaching."

That left too much room for my imagination, so I pressed him further.

"What teaching?" Of the young girls, I imagined.

"I was voted out of teaching…for now." He was looking straight forward but added those last two words with emphasis.

"How is that?"

"The sponsors at the *Conservatorio* voted seven to six against me." Antonio knew that the Trapensi house had a vote, but he didn't ask how we had voted. Truthfully, I didn't know, since my father tended to such affairs.

"What does that mean for you?"

With a careful wave of his hand, Antonio dismissed the importance of the vote.

"It's a regular thing. They do it every year."

"They vote you out every year?" I asked. I was not being harsh or ridiculous. I actually didn't know how the voting process went, although as soon as I had said the words I realized that it must have seemed that I was making fun at his expense.

"No," he replied emphatically. "They vote every year; not vote me out." And after a moment's pause that allowed for another gulp of wine, he added, "They will vote again and I will be back."

With that, Antonio stood suddenly, grasped the glass to drain its contents, and swung around to leave.

* * *

The timing of the vote came at a complicated time. Antonio was rising in the view of the public, and his contracts to perform were growing, so his compositions and his performances were well regarded. I inquired as to whether his dismissal was due to some scandalous behavior but found nothing to support such a conclusion.

I also asked my father how he had voted and he was curt.

"Of course I voted against him," he said without raising his face from the book he was reading. "He's a scallywag, and we don't need men like him around our young girls."

Despite my admitted jealousies, I thought my father's opinion was uncalled for. Antonio was known in some circles as a gadabout and too loose in some respects, but most of the stories that were told had the distinct air of exaggeration. Some even carried a tone of fantasy, reflecting the desires of the orator more than the behavior of the subject.

I was also able to find out more about the voting process. It was conducted each year for each teacher. Normally, the process was a mundane affair, more a repetitive vote of confidence than a true test of quality or character. But the process allowed for those with votes – usually only the benefactors of *L'Ospedale* – to reprimand someone that they disapproved of.

I was not able to discover the identity of the others who had voted against Antonio, but I suspected that they shared my father's opinion and had shunned the *maestro* due to the stories about his public and private behavior.

The complications of timing had to do with another related, but independent event that occurred just one month before the vote. Antonio Vivaldi had secured another contract to publish a collection of his compositions, his second at this point. They were mostly concertos for violin and *basso continuo,* and would be managed by Antonio Bortoli, a local Venetian publisher, which he announced publicly as Opus 2. I understood the marketing value of such nomenclature. Instead of giving name to the work, such as *Il Sole del Veneto* or some such other title, naming it Opus 2 made the public aware of the continuing nature of the violinist's career and the fact that another notebook was also available for sale.

This notebook sparked great interest in Venice and beyond almost as soon as it was announced. So, income from it filled in the gap of that lost from Antonio's service at the *Conservatorio.* In fact, it probably drew the ire of *L'Ospedale's* benefactors who thought their vote to expunge the musician would serve as a difficult penalty for him.

On the heels of the publication of Opus 2 and his newfound freedom from the routine of teaching, Antonio devoted his time to freelance performances, drawing even more income than from the sales of the notebook and spreading his name and reputation throughout northern Italy.

May 1711
Venice and Brescia

The excitement of getting Antonio to perform grew over the months since his dismissal from the *Conservatorio*. With more free time, a recent publication of a new notebook, and the word-of-mouth advertising that followed every performance that he gave, he was more in demand than ever and I wondered each time that I saw him in the streets of Venice how long it might be before he would make his next appearance in the city.

Those who managed the *Conservatorio* also noticed. They saw that the expulsion – instead of punishing the man – had freed him to make more money and spread his fame. They also noticed how the students whom he left behind mourned his absence. The young girls were accustomed to sharing the room with this renowned musician – not to mention certain other unspeakable actions not appropriate for this journal – and they were distraught that he would be gone forever.

Earlier this month, the benefactors were pressed to vote once again on Antonio's place as a teacher.

He won this vote unanimously, but then had to be coaxed back to the position. Having established himself as a performing musician and a composer in high demand, it wasn't immediately clear that he would welcome a return to teaching.

But one evening, I saw him at the Café Ridolfo at his usual table. Instead of the two or three mature women that were normally seated with him, I noticed a not very small collection of pubescent girls circled around his table. The collective numbered about ten, and they looked to range in age from thirteen to eighteen, and I took them right away to be students from his class. The circle of pretty young things with their innocent smiles and lovely dresses was obviously brought together to draw Antonio back into the web of the *Conservatorio's* faculty, and I could see by the color in his cheeks and the pleased smile on his face that the tactic had been successful.

* * *

Several weeks later, Filipe returned to Venice. He said that he was here on important family business, but his furtive smile led me to believe that this 'family business' meant that he was abandoning his family back in Marseilles to visit his *amour* who lived just off the great canal in a modest cluster of old homes near the Ponte degli Scalzi.

"I heard Vivaldi recently, along with his father, but the old man could not keep up with the style of the son."

"Where?"

"They were in Brescia. I don't know if they're still there, but they – or should I say he – was called by the people of the town to perform and, perhaps offer some new composition that they could say was created for their little town."

Antonio was now more than thirty years old and instead of following his father along for opportunities, the roles were now reversed, with the aging barber following his son in hopes of extending his own modest musical career.

"He was stupendous!" said Filipe excitedly. "You really should come to see him."

My friend knew of the strained relationship between Antonio and me, although I had to confess that the *maestro* himself did little to aggravate it. The distance between us – verily, the simmering anger that hung between us – was mostly of my own creation. While standing with Antonio I could be pleasant, if short, but when away from him or when witnessing his antics in the middle of an adoring crowd I felt resentful. He was the musician that I wanted to be. Even worse, his talent was so great that he could pull off masterful performances with ease, performances that I knew I could never reach even with years of practice.

My thoughts went to Antonio and Filipe droned on. The adulation of the girls who followed the *maestro* everywhere and bathed him in selfless love bothered me, but I was not seeking the companionship of little girls. I was still not married but counted on my station in life and my position in Venetian society to secure me an appropriate wife when the time was right.

Filipe knew that I seldom watched Antonio perform even when he was in my own city. In fact, I believe I saw him on the violin more often in the studio with these indulgent girls than I did in the Basilica or in some concert hall. He had many paid performances, true, but I wasn't one of the paying customers.

Instead, I was going to the *Conservatorio* more than in the past, assessing the benefit of the money that my father gave the program. But I was also drawn there by the presence of one particular girl.

Rachel d'Invito was now eleven years old and although her family did not need to count on the services of *L'Ospedale* which mostly served the poor and orphaned of Venice, they recognized a budding talent in the girl on the violin and the pianoforte. Ludovico d'Invito wanted to encourage that virtue in his daughter, and his wife Mariella agreed. So, Rachel had begun to take regular lessons in the *Conservatorio*.

Even at this precious age, the young girl showed great beauty and promise for womanhood. She had a radiant smile – present since birth – silky hair and perfectly smooth skin. The first time I saw her in the music room I blushed with excitement but composed myself quickly. It would be a scandal if a grown man showed flushed cheeks at the site of a girl who had not yet been visited by her womanly assignment.

Or had she?

I peered around the corner once again and listened intently as she lightly stroked the keys of the pianoforte. Even my untrained ear could tell that it was not an expert or inspired rendition, but the softness of the melody and the way that the notes hung in the air impressed me greatly.

Fortunately, Rachel was not assigned to Antonio's studio. She took her lessons from an old man with thin gray hair and wrinkled skin. A man who, despite the appearance of age, when he sat at the bench could still play the instrument with strength and emotion. He was a perfect match for the young lady that I admired from afar. The old teacher was talented in music, but unappealing in his visage. I – well – I was a man older than Rachel with an infirm leg, but great promise in the world of merchants who controlled the fate of Venice.

In my reverie, I forgot that Filipe was still there in front of me. The sound of his voice had lowered while I entertained my fantasies, but he was still talking when my consciousness returned.

"And you should," he said, in conclusion.

I had missed some of Filipe's rendition of the performance but tuned back in to his voice just in time for him to tell me about Antonio's new composition.

"*Stabat Mater* he called it. It was simple and predictable, but the way he made the violin strings hum the melody was amazing."

My friend could see that my attention was elsewhere, so he patted me once on the shoulder and turned to go.

November 1711
Venice and Amsterdam

Antonio didn't let his recall to the *Conservatorio* slow the pace of his writing. If *Stabat Mater* was "simple and predictable" as Filipe described – I still have not heard it performed – his next production was anything but.

I heard him play the lead violin part alone while he practiced in his studio, then just last week I was able to hear the full complement of strings for which *L'estro armonico* was written. It was performed in a small studio on the second floor of one of Venice's richest families. I had been invited as a guest of the family to a special dinner to celebrate the graduation of their daughter – I have forgotten her name – from music studies at the *Conservatorio*. Graduation might not be the right word. The pleasant looking young woman had attracted the attention of numerous suitors so her parents decided that continuing education in music was unnecessary. Their plan was to marry her off.

The music room in their apartment was a perfect setting, with its high ceiling, stone walls draped with tapestries, and soft carpet covering the wooden planks to soften the sounds. In that setting we could appreciate the lilting music of the composition under the soft glow of the candles that twinkled on the mantle and side tables.

I stood throughout the performance staring out the broad window at the undulating water of the canal below as gondolas drifted by. Even without staring at the small assembly of musicians, I could always pick out the part played by Antonio. True, he reserved for himself the best segments of every composition, but it was his perfect balance and evocation of notes that identified the *maestro* among the plebeians seated around him.

L'estro armonico was written as a collection of concertos for strings. Labelled Opus 3, it was unlike his first two published compositions. Opus 1 was written for violin and *basso continuo*, although this latter instrument was only used for background and structure. Opus 2 was written solely for violin. Expert though it was, the range and complexity of the piece was limited by isolation to that single instrument. In Opus 3, Antonio gave the cello an important role, added the viola, and repeated the role of the *basso continuo* to demonstrate anew the genius that he possesses. Somehow, he manages to meld complexity with simplicity so that a whole new world of music seems to arise from the orchestration.

I stood, hands clasped behind my back. I kept my eyes focused on the canal traffic below and the flickering of candles in the homes across the water. The whisper of the violin and the intoned measures of the cello wrapped me in a musical comfortour. The notes veritably breathed, soft and easy at times, breathless and huffing at others. Antonio had worked in some pauses, tense moments of complete silence, and I smiled when one occurred. He was truly a master, and he knew that some compositions needed a single blank space of utter quiet to draw the listeners into rapt attention. Then the strings of both violin and cello would leap back into that void and the hearts of listeners around the room would skip a beat and then race into action in time with the music.

Five, six...eleven, twelve. I counted the concertos as they were performed and when the pause after the twelfth remained longer than the rest, the small private audience politely clapped their approval. I spun around just in time to catch a slight frown on Antonio's face, showing his disappointment with the light applause – this was typical of the cultured deportment of such an exclusive audience – probably because it did not satisfy him. But the twitch I detected at the left corner of his mouth quickly disappeared and he turned to thank his host with all the aplomb of a man who still sought favor among the moneyed class of Venice.

Which, in fact, was Antonio's *raison d'être* for composing this work.

He was now thirty-three years old and in search of a benefactor. He had proven his worth in both composition and performance, had won sought-after positions at the *Conservatorio* and in distant cities, and it seemed that this was the time for him to be awarded a sinecure with some powerful king or prince, a position that would allow him to concentrate his full powers on writing music and not earning money on which to live.

Just days after he performed for that private audience, Antonio was called upon by the city's fathers to produce *L'estro armonico* again, this time in a larger space and open to ticket-buying customers. When the announcement was made for the date and time, the billboard carried Antonio's name in large letters, under which was the name of the composition in similar type, and then under that a dedication to the Grand Prince Ferdinando of Tuscany, a member of the powerful Medici family – in fact, the eldest son of Cosimo III himself – who sought to restore the centrality of the family in the southern states, power which his father had seemed to fritter away in a series of poor decisions.

But Ferdinando still had money and stature and had already reached contracts with some of our great musicians. It is said that he dabbled in music himself, learning the pianoforte and attempting to play some stringed instruments, and it was probably his disappointment in his own limitations that drove him to sponsor other great musicians. Rumors abound that he preferred male musicians not just for their soft handling of their instruments, but for their soft handling of his.

Antonio knew all this without traveling to Tuscany. News traveled on the waves to Venice just as fine silks reached our shores, and we knew as much about the affairs of Ferdinando as did the Tuscan *paesani* who lived near him.

Antonio's plan was simple, yet brilliant. By dedicating the new arrangement to an absent prince – and I was quite sure that he would send copies of the broadside to Ferdinando – he would entice the prince to order a performance. Ferdinando's insistence on the best of all artists would leave him unsatisfied with any local musicians, adding to his fervor to see Antonio perform in person. And to get the *maestro* to travel to Tuscany to see him, the prince would have to enter into a contract of support.

So, after this second rendition of *L'estro armonico,* I expected my friend to take a leave of absence from the *Conservatorio* to explore his options in the south. His farewell from Venice was a grand affair, although he put on airs about keeping his departure quiet. There were several nights running when Antonio could be seen holding court at Café Ridolfo, at times in the company of adult women who sat primly around him in twos and threes, at times in a giggling crowd of young girls with wide eyes and unselfconscious smiles.

The older women would lean in to Antonio, bend forward to the advantage of their bounteous breasts, or shift their hips suggestively to indicate later plans. The little girls would only turn their little smiles and blushing cheeks toward the man.

One evening, Antonio was sitting alone with a strikingly beautiful woman whom I did not recognize. Her shiny black hair was held in tight curls on her forehead, as a long train of braided hair cascaded down over her collar. In fact, I noticed with some excitement that her collar was quite low on the back of her neck, and the front neckline swung daringly close to her bosom, exposing more of her femininity than would be proper in Venetian society. Had her deportment not be impeccable, I might have taken this siren for a lady of the night.

On his last evening in our city, Antonio held court among about half a dozen young female students of his. They were the older ones in his class, perhaps all sixteen years old or thereabouts since the time was late and the younger girls would already be in bed. Except for one.

Signora d'Invito stood at the fringe of this little crowd and watched Antonio from that short distance. Her left hand hung at her side and enclosed the fingers of her daughter Rachel who was radiant as always. I saw the way the girl stared in awe at the *maestro* and the muscles tightened around my heart. I had come to distrust Antonio's intentions with women and girls, and this particular one held me in rapture.

At that thought, I paused and probably blushed, so I turned away. The realization that Rachel had such a hold on me, this little thing of eleven years old, frightened and excited me all at once.

Not able to get complete control of my feelings, I chose to leave the café scene and return to my office by the quay.

* * *

Soon after Antonio's departure for Tuscany, a notebook of *L'estro armónico* was published in Amsterdam by Estienne Roger which almost immediately rose to great success. I ordered a copy from a business associate in Amsterdam and when it arrived I could readily see why the full orchestration was so impressive. I could not play the violin anymore without incurring the wrath of my father, but he wouldn't know that I had remained fluent in reading music.

May 1712
Venice

Dario met me in the office by the docks this afternoon to discuss the shipments that would be received this week. With my father's diminished health and his tendency to spend more time in his private quarters, I would have expected our agent to engage me more in the business and treat me more with the respect due to the owner of a large company.

But it wasn't like that. Dario trusted my father for all the decisions and as the old man grew weak and removed himself from daily operations of the Trapensi house, Dario simply took on more independent authority, often advising me of his own decisions rather than asking for mine.

This troubled me for a while, but I had to admit to myself that I wasn't really interested in business. I enjoyed the returns and spent the money and took pleasure in having the finest clothes and housing, but the quotidian affairs of business were a distraction that I would rather leave to someone else. Dario seemed like the logical pick, so I didn't interfere as

I watched him take more and more control of the Trapensi import business.

I have turned thirty-four years of age and began considering my life. The family business would insure me against any financial threats of the future, whether I wrested control from Dario or simply let him continue to manage it.

Music was receding in my thoughts, at least my active participation in it. So, I had neither business nor music to consume my time. I was not yet married, although a man of my position could wait longer than the working peasants of our society who needed to father a gaggle of children to carry on the labors of their simple life.

Fathering children could wait, for me. Instead, I could follow in the footsteps of other well-funded men of my class and entertain the hours of the day with many women. Until I chose the one to bear my children with. But as I thought about my life to date, there had not been many such women. Only two, in fact. I wondered what was the cause of my poor experience in that department. I am not particularly handsome, although not unseemly looking. I enjoy a fair sense of humor, although at times my levity falls flat. My gimpy leg bothers me both physically and emotionally, but that should not stand in the way of a man of great family.

Shyness is a weakness, to be sure, but I am not so shy that I would go mute in the company of a fine woman. I am well educated and, although I have been dissuaded from playing a musical instrument, I can hold my own in a discussion of the finer points of music and orchestration.

"And this is the next one," I heard Dario's voice say. It drew me out of my self-evaluation.

"Yes. Quite so," I replied absently trying to sound engaged in the discussion. Dario was pointing to the docks with one hand and to the ledger on the table in front of us with his other. The ship flew the Trapensi flag on the mast just below the bright colors of the Venetian pennant, and the way it sat low in the water promised a large cargo of valuables. The deckhands were tying it up and pulling the hull closer to the dock, and their glistening muscles could be seen to strain as far up as the window that I peered from.

"It includes wheat from the south, jewels from the east, and oil from everywhere," my manager explained. I wondered why the oil would come from everywhere but when I looked at Dario's smile, I decided that he was making fun and hoped to catch me in his riddle. I declined to speak.

Dario returned to his ledger and made marks in it about the size, type, and quantity of the import. I wondered how he already knew of the contents of the ship, but recalled that faster boats brought news every day, including reports of what the cargo ships would bring to our port. I knew that he would check his numbers when the imports were unloaded on the docks, and that was why Dario was paid by us.

After a moment of watching him tend to our books, I turned to leave the room. Out of the corner of my eye, I saw Dario stand back from the desk and turn to face me.

"Sire," he began. "I understand that the city fathers are celebrating the *Festa della Sensa* this day and tomorrow."

This I knew. The *Festa* was an annual event and a fantastic display of Venetian people, art, and costume. Some say it rivals the great masked *Carnevale* that also occurs each year.

"The *Festa* will draw crowds from all over the region, all over Italy. There will be jesters, acrobats, artists, performers, and visitors to crowd our streets and piazzas.

"And there will be many beautiful women," he added, then paused.

"Your lordship deserves a woman of high standing…and money. Perhaps the *Festa* will be enjoyable for you," Dario suggested, with little hint of subtlety.

He was right about all that. I recalled from times past that the great canal and all the smaller waterways of Venice would be crowded with gondolas and other craft, some carrying colorful flags aloft and others simply packed with singing patrons who were enjoying the wine and spirits of the day. The streets of the city were also packed with crowds of people, both Venetians and outsiders, and the bridges that curled above the canals served both as viewing spots and travel corridors, so that sometimes moving as little distance as from my office to the Ponte Rialto would take over an hour.

The one thing that stood out each year was the tremendous display of color. Venetians were known for bright yellows, greens, blues, and hues of red, and on days of the *Festa* all these shades stretched across the viewing horizon so that no modest grays or whites – such as the colors of the buildings in along the side streets of Venice – could be seen among the swath of brilliance.

I didn't want to admit to his wisdom, even with a nod of my head, so I turned curtly about and left the room without a farewell.

I retired to my quarters to consider Dario's words. It was indeed the right time for me to find a suitable woman and to marry. My father had settled on my mother when he was of thirty-four years, just as I am now. The possibilities in Venice as far as the market for wives was good, although I had flitted about the edges of noble society for so long that I feared I might, by now, have been taken as an afterthought. I would have to be more outgoing and dress the part of a man in search of a wife, attend the parties with a purpose and show off my assets and noble position. I would cut a handsome figure, dressed out in finery and sporting a cape of gold-embroidered satin.

Or I could be taken as a comic impersonator, I feared. My shoulders slumped at the thought. Although a man of means and stature, I did not inhabit the circle of preeners and *bon vivants*, those of quick wit and high voice. And I had no specific skill that set me apart from the others.

I would make a go of it, though, attend the parties and events in the *Festa della Sensa*, ride in a hired gondola and let the world see me. And after each day's attempts at society, I would retire to my quarters once again.

* * *

On the first day of *Festa*, I left my office on the quay and walked through the crowded streets toward the Piazza San Marco. The festival atmosphere and ceaseless sound of music and chatter filled the air and I was quite unable to suppress a smile.

Just as I turned the corner around the Palazzo del Doge, I saw Signora d'Invito. She had her son Brie and daughter Rachel by her side, and her smile beamed at the crowd and festivities around her. The signora was focused on the horns that blared and jesters who danced and produced magic tricks, but I held her and her family in my gaze.

Her husband, Ludovico d'Invito, seldom appeared in public and almost never with his family. He was a man whose success depended on constant attention to his business. Unlike mine, whose estate was secured by two generations of profits, d'Invito's could only be grown and insured by intense and unremitting focus on the affairs of the day.

His wife, however, and children would be free to entertain themselves at Venice's environs. The plays, symphonies, art displays, and festivals would be their routine experience, and Signora d'Invito was focused on enjoying these things and introducing her children to them.

The boy, Brie, was getting a little too old to remain by his mother's side, but little Rachel was in her element. Now at the age of twelve, she was showing the physical signs of female maturity, and retained the rosy cheeks and innocent visage of childhood.

"*Buon giorno*," Signora d'Invito said as I approached.

"*Buon giorno*," I replied. "How are you today?" I asked but addressed both mother and daughter in the query. Brie stood stoically by. He was polite and reserved and seemed ambivalently well-mannered in his twin roles as son and as young man escorting his family in public.

"Are you enjoying the *Festa*?" I inquired of Rachel. Her mother beamed at her pretty daughter, expectant of a refined and womanly reply.

"Yes, sir," was all the girl had to say, but the little comment was accompanied by a slight curtsy and bowed head. Her mother smiled at Rachel and then addressed me.

"And you, sir, are you well?"

"Quite so," was my quick response, although I stood leaning on my good foot to disguise the limp in my left leg.

"The Festa is such a marvelous sight," she added. "So much color! Each year I wait for these days with anticipation. It seems like the entire world is on display here."

I agreed with the signora but had nothing to add, so I remained silent. As they bid their goodbye, Rachel offered a smile and a wave, and I responded in kind.

July 1713
Venice and Vicenza

There was a buzz of news at the docks this afternoon. News that Antonio Vivaldi was returning to Venice dominated the reports, at least that which did not apply to imports of valuable goods, and talk arose of his success in Vicenza two months past.

In his musical passage through the cities of Italy, Antonio had drawn praise for his published works and his performances, but the locals were always pressing him to create something new, something that they could call their own. That fact strikes me as odd since all of his compositions would belong to him, not the peasantry of the villages. But still, in the adoration of the *maestro*, they persisted.

So, it came about that while in Vicenza this past May, Antonio wrote an opera. This in itself is a great matter for him. He was not an opera virtuoso but with each bleat of the citizen sheep, he stretched his genius beyond his last frontier and entered upon a new one. This opera, called *Ottone in Villa,* was performed at the Teatro delle Grazie in Vicenza using the lyrics of one Sebastiano Biancardi, not a man I am familiar with. I had seen neither the score nor the libretto, but Venice's fervor for their favorite son was such that the story was retold from mouth to ear across our island and reached my hearing by nightfall.

The opera involves a Roman saga and four individuals who are caught in a complicated set of romantic relationships. According to the reports I have received, the emperor – on whom the work is named, Ottone – is in love with a woman who is, herself, in love with two men. One of the men turns out to be a woman, who is in love with the other man. Of course, love among men and women and men and men is common, and women and women also, so I wasn't scandalized by the story. But the third-hand reports that reached me confused the telling and I couldn't understand who was whom. Perhaps I'll have a chance to see it myself if Antonio permits its performance in Venice.

Now, he is back in our city and enjoying the popular acclaim that has become common for him. I saw him briefly this afternoon in the halls of the Palazzo del Doge. He was in a small circle of men, and a pretty woman had her hand slipped through the crook of Antonio's arm.

"*Buon giorno*, Signor Vivaldi," I said, choosing a more formal greeting since he was in the company of others.

"Ah, Domenico," he replied gaily. "How are you, my friend?" But true to the Antonio that I knew so well, he didn't wait for a reply from me.

"Do you know Signora Ristaldi?"

I noticed that he introduced the woman clinging to his arm as 'signora,' not 'signorina.'

"No," I began. "I haven't had the pleasure," I said, removing my hat and offering a slight bow in her direction.

"She sang the part of Ostilio in my opera. Isn't she beautiful?"

"*Si*, quite so," I replied, although his focus on her physical talents gave little evidence of her vocal talents.

"But isn't Ostilio a man in your opera?"

"*Si*," Antonio intoned with the reverence of a creative artist, "but the part is shared by two."

I was confused by his misdirection, and he picked up on that.

"Ostilio poses as a man, but is truly a woman, who falls in love with a man in the opera."

The loose use of sexual identification seemed to delight Antonio, and I saw him press his fingers gently into the sleeved arm of Signora Ristaldi as he described it to me. For a moment, I wondered whether the woman before me was a man, or both.

I paid my respects to all present, bowed once again to the signora, and lifted my hat back onto my head.

"I hope to see the opera one day. Perhaps you will entertain your own people with this masterpiece," I said. "Or write another for your Venetians."

"Yes," he chuckled, "they are mine, aren't they?"

I left them there and heard a light titter behind my back. As the blood rose in my cheeks, I reminded myself of what a rogue Antonio could be, especially when he was using me as the target of his humor.

At times, I upbraided myself for falling for Antonio's jibes. I knew that it would be best to smile back and return the evil tribute, but my humor often failed me in the moment when it was most needed.

November 1714
Venice

Antonio remained in Venice through the winter and spring of this year, and he resumed his teaching post at the *Conservatorio*. After his sojourn in Vicenza and parts more distant, he was welcomed by his students with applause and the expected level of adolescent admiration. At times, that admiration showed signs of lust among the older girls, a fact which continued to bother me on my visits to the school.

On one particular afternoon, I passed by the old man's studio where Rachel took her lessons and listened intently from outside the doorway. I could tell that the number of girls within had grown over the month and that old man who conducted the lessons had his hands full with the differing levels of competence and practice among them. The girls in his charge were not as experienced in music as those assigned to Antonio, owing in part to the old man's limited skills as a teacher, and I wondered how Rachel was doing.

After a respectful pause in my obscure post outside the room, I turned toward the door to face the class straight on. I quickly surveyed the room since I had little interest in the music or the gaggle of girls. I wanted to find Rachel and enjoy her pretty presence for a moment. But I soon realized that she was not there. She could have been out that day, perhaps with the periodic ailment that afflicts girls of her age. To satisfy my curiosity, I walked down the hallway to Antonio's room. There was only a handful of girls in there since his advanced study would be limited to those with great promise.

There sat Rachel in a chair just near Antonio. She held the violin up to her chin and posed with the bow just above the strings.

"This way," he instructed her. "Your wrist should be above the bow so that your fingers dangle below it."

Rachel shifted the position of her right hand and looked at Antonio for approval. He reached out for her hand and repositioned the girl's fingers, seeming to pull against a reluctance woven into the sinews of her hand.

"Let go," he said, and she dropped her hand to her lap.

"No, I mean let go of the bow, but pose your hand above it. I will arrange it for you."

I knew from my own struggle with the violin the importance of relaxing with the bow. A too-strong grip would make the strings squeak; a too-lose grip would let the bow wobble and the notes come out as hollow or weak.

"Yes, this way," he said with a smile. Rachel had slowly grasped his meaning and was doing better. The sounds coming from her instrument proved that her skill was advancing.

Antonio stepped around Rachel's right shoulder, away from the shoulder on which her violin was perched and stroked her hair as he stroked her ego.

"Yes, this is much better," he said, and Rachel blushed with the glow of accomplishment. Or was she blushing from his touch?

I turned around in the doorway and marched out of the place immediately. I had seen Antonio's effect on women and girls for a long time, but I couldn't tolerate that behavior with Rachel.

* * *

I was drawn back to the *Conservatorio* just a few days later. By now, I had lost my pretense of checking on the Trapensi investment in *L'Ospedale* but couldn't resist the urge to visit the premises with frequency. On this visit, I went straight to Antonio's studio to see if Rachel was safe there. And in my hurry, I didn't pause at the threshold but strode directly into the chamber. Antonio was in the middle of a lesson but stopped when I entered.

"*Buon giorno*, Domenico. What brings you here on this fine day?"

Instead of replying, I quickly scanned the small group of girls but didn't see Rachel. She was not there at all.

Suddenly, I was terrified by the thought that I would be discovered in my longing for this young girl. I had not spoken of her to anyone but Antonio had seen me in his room just recently and might make the connection. Before he could blurt something out about my attraction to the girl, I rushed from the room.

When I had retreated to a safe spot, I leaned against the wall and appraised the situation. My heart was still racing from nearly being discovered, and I wanted to collect my thoughts and my feelings before proceeding. A bit farther down the hallway was the old man's studio and I could hear the sound of instruments being plucked, strummed, and keyed, so I went in that direction. To my surprise,

Rachel was in that room, returned to the old man's instruction, demoted from Antonio's studio.

In an evil moment, I wondered what test Rachel had failed to be returned to the beginner's level of instruction. I had not heard her music at any length, so I couldn't assess that as the reason. I believed in her virtue, though, and grew angry at the thought that Antonio had dispensed with her due to Rachel's failure of another type of test.

* * *

Just this month, a broadside appeared in the piazzas of Venice announcing a new opera. Antonio Vivaldi was listed as the composer and Grazio Braccioli as the librettist. Although there was no mention of it on the poster, Antonio's father had a hand in the production. Considering the reversal of fortunes for father and son, it might have been Antonio trying once again to give his father an opportunity.

The production was titled *Orlando Finto Pazzo* – Orlando, the Crazy One – and was performed at the Teatro Sant'Angelo, near the Ponte Rialto. I attended on the second night but was disappointed in the music, the lyrics…just about everything. I carefully examined my motives to see if my growing disgust with Vivaldi was the root of my opinion, but upon hearing other spectators openly discuss the deficits of the opera, I can honestly hold to my own assessment of its failure.

As it turned out, I would not have seen the opera had I waited a while longer. The sponsors of the production cancelled it after only a handful of performances.

Antonio was clearly unmoored by the failure of this latest venture. He locked himself away in his apartment; according to rumor, he even locked himself up in his very chamber, denying even his siblings access to him. Music could be heard coming from the room at odd hours over the days that followed until one day he emerged, white-skinned and even thinner of body and bone than before.

A normal routine resumed for him and, over the next two weeks, he overcame the pallor and filled out the belt around his trousers. He was back at the *Conservatorio* and was heard performing some new piece while resting between lessons. I saw him once or twice and got a brief wave in recognition, but he was very focused on organizing his thoughts about the notes.

On another visit I saw Rachel practicing the violin in the old man's studio. She was performing a simple piece on the violin and I enjoyed the sound of it produced by her own hand. I thought about her short tenure in Antonio's studio and was ambivalent about the outcome. Had she remained with the *maestro* I would have worried about her welfare; but her transfer to the old man's instruction created a sense of sadness at her being rejected.

I listened attentively for a moment until she looked up and caught my eye. She smiled at me without losing her concentration and I returned the gesture, no doubt with a little redness in my cheeks at being noticed. When another girl sitting nearby giggled, I thought it was at me, the old man with a gimpy leg, so I left the scene and walked down the hallway.

Before long, Antonio's focus produced another set of concertos which he titled *La Stravaganza*. They were written primarily for violin, although he followed his earlier pattern of including other stringed instruments for structure. Once again, it was a series of twelve concertos, in which ten of the compositions were arranged in three movements each; one of the sonatas had two movements and another one had four.

The artistry displayed in *La Stravaganza* renewed Antonio's spirit and his reputation. Operas could generate more income, with their theatres full of paying guests, but after the premature demise of *Orlando Finto Pazzo* he needed to have his faith restored. The reception he got for *La Stravaganza* was what he had hoped for, and so I expected that he would abandon future attempts at opera.

April 1715
Venice

There is something that I do not understand about musicians. Their ego must be the energy that propels them forward because, despite my prediction that he would abandon plans for any more operas, Antonio forged ahead. As soon as his ego was restored by the success of *La Stravaganza* – and I made a mental note of his choice of name for it – he went into a feverish routine of writing and produced another opera in only a few months.

Nerone Fatto Cesare was a dramatic piece that he wrote, arranged, and performed in Venice in the spring of this year. And to test his own reputation, he even dared to have it billed at the Teatro Sant'Angelo, the hall where we witnessed the sagging failure that he presented once before.

And, yet, how can I doubt Antonio? The new opera was a wild success. I concluded that it was because he had lowered expectations with the presentation of *Orlando Finto Pazzo;* however, others were more effusive in their praise.

On the evening following the opening, when the actors would rest their voices for a return performance two days hence, Antonio could be seen in a small throng of admirers, mostly women, including many girls. He was striding lazily through the Piazza San Marco, walking slowly enough that his coterie of followers could maintain the ringlet around him.

I nodded as he passed by but, when I caught his eye, Antonio paused, then swerved in my direction. I was torn between sharing the glow of excitement that permeated his crowd and the fear of being embarrassed by one of his personal barbs.

"Domenico!" he hailed as he approached. I saw a tall woman, taller than Antonio himself, walking closest to him and pressing her bosom against his arm at every opportunity. I also noticed a half dozen or so young girls, even the youngest ones permitted in his class, clinging to the edges of the throng. There were pretty little things in brightly colored dresses and innocent smiles, and the older more mature women dressed to display their greatest assets and eager to win some attention from the *maestro*. My curiosity got the best of me and I searched the faces for that of Rachel. She was not in this mob, and I relaxed at the thought.

"I saw you in the seats at my latest opera," he continued. "Thank you for spending some time to hear my composition."

He paused for theatrical effect.

"And what did you think?" I said, impertinently turning the tables on him. The words slipped from my mouth before I could realize what I was saying, but I was pleased at my wit. In effect, I was asking the *maestro* what he thought of his own work, instead of him asking me what I thought of the production.

Antonio smiled slyly at me, recognizing the way in which my question had precluded his attempt at humor.

"I thought it was grand!" he replied to the polite cheers from his circle of women.

"And what will you do next?" I asked. I noticed that my ostentatious first query had drawn the attention of the females around him, and I enjoyed my new position. In fact, I was standing on the second step of the colonnade, just in front of the Café Ridolfo and Antonio was still on the cobblestones of the piazza, so I held the higher position, almost as a royal member might address someone of lower rank.

"I will write more operas!" he said with brightness and intensity.

Then, waving his hand above his head before dropping it to brush lightly against the flirtatious woman's breast, he turned away toward the center of the piazza and the crowd pinwheeled around him and followed in like manner.

* * *

For all the pomp and splendor of Antonio's return to prominence, there was a gray, darker side to his life. A few days after the encounter in Piazza San Marco, I walked past three men that I knew from the city's magistracy. I nodded my head and tapped the brim of my hat in salute and, although one of them offered a thin smile in reply, the others continued their whispered conversation, pausing only briefly as I passed by the group.

I could hear some words of theirs – in my position, it was assumed that I would protect the established order, so I was no threat – and Antonio Vivaldi came up, along with the name Domenico Lalli. I knew the pseudonym for the librettist in Antonio's *Ottone in Villa,* so I assumed that the clandestine conversation had to do with the production of music. I knew that musical well from reports of its production in Vicenza, and I was familiar with the scandalous gossip about the relations portrayed between men therein, so I came away from this quiet conversation assuming the men, all older than me, were arguing about the unnatural display of cultic love in the story.

Out on the cobblestones, I happened upon another impromptu discussion among a clutch of younger people. They did not speak in whispers and paid me no attention as I went by, so I was able to catch more of what they were saying. According to their report, a new opera by Vivaldi and Lalli had been banned by the elders of Venice, and so the *maestro* was shopping elsewhere to put on the production. I tarried beside a fisherman's cart to try to glean more of the story and heard one youth say with a laugh, "They will let the men love…"

"But not here," interrupted his friend to laughter from his companions.

"I mean the men of *Ottone*," he said, completing his sentence.

"No, the people of Vicenza allowed *Ottone* to be shown, and they allowed men to love…"

"Yes," the first one struck back, "but they will never allow the women to be seen in adulterous positions."

"You mean the people of Vicenza, yes?"

"Or Venice. Perhaps the people of Vicenza will allow it…"

"Will they be shown in arms?" another asked.

"I do not know, but the people of Vicenza will allow it; not our old goats here in Venice."

"So!" one declared with his hand held high, "we go to Vicenza!" and he was rewarded with a round of laughter and clapping.

* * *

I was intrigued by these conversations and went in search of more information. It would be another two days before I found someone with knowledge of the rumored campaign.

"Dario," I said, confiding in my agent in a way that made me feel nervous. "What is the city saying about Antonio Vivaldi these days."

"That he is finished," came the reply. Dario barely looked up from the paperwork while he responded to my question.

"But, how could that be? He just produced a wonderful success. *Nerone fatto Cesare* was acclaimed by critics and the public alike."

"The elders have their say."

"And they liked it too. I didn't have to inquire; there was a general round of applause for the production."

"It's about *Ottone in Villa*," he countered.

"That opera was performed in Vicenza, not here. What do the elders care about that?"

At mention of the previous opera, Dario laid down his quill and addressed me directly.

"It is about neither *Nerone fatto Cesare* nor *Ottone in Villa,* although the latter one may have laid him open to criticism."

I wondered why, and what was the connection to Venice, but I waited for Dario to say more.

"He and Lalli, the one who wrote the story and lyrics for *Ottone* have collaborated on another opera, something called *Arsilda, Regina di Ponto.*"

"And?"

"Arsilda is a woman who is in love with another woman," he explained while staring directly at me. As men of this age, we were familiar with ribald tales of men loving men and women loving women, and on the small dark stages of the *cantine* around the city, peasants would be regaled with their stories. Vivaldi was known to have some unspoken proclivities, so the production of an opera that focused on two women should not have caused such a stir.

"The city elders banned the opera," Dario continued. "They have ruled that such a thing is an abomination and would not be performed in this city."

"So, is Antonio in some sort of trouble with the city?"

"No, but he is angry at the decision. There is talk of him offering it elsewhere, and even talk of Signor Vivaldi moving elsewhere and abandoning Venice.

In the weeks that followed, the talk of Antonio's new creation – and of Antonio himself – died down. I saw him at the Café Ridolfo and at other places around the city. His mood seemed to have evened out and he appeared to have returned to his routine pursuits. I took the time to visit the *Conservatorio* and I found him in the salon teaching the young girls the piano and violin, so I dropped the incident from my memory.

October 1716
Venice

Antonio has remained in our city for the past year, continuing his classes and being followed about the streets by his adoring clique of fawning young girls. He is reported – on a too frequent basis by the wagging tongues of Venice – as being seen in the arms of one of those girls in public places. At times, of more than one.

I remained in my place of business and remained unmarried, but this time I had made certain decisions about my life. I could no longer pretend to not have a deep interest in Rachel d'Invito and she, at sixteen years old, could perceive some of my intent. So could her mother. Rachel's attendance at the *Conservatorio* was lessened somewhat by her entry into womanhood; it was now important for her parents to find the appropriate spouse for her, and their search for such a solution gave me grave concern.

She should be mine, I admitted secretly, and when I caught her eye and was rewarded with a smile, I convinced myself that she agreed. But I would have to find some way to enter my name in the contest for her hand.

I visited Ludovico d'Invito one day at his place of business, encouraging a more settled arrangement between our houses and ensuring that my person would be thought of frequently and favorably. I confabulated an excuse to visit their home, saying that I needed to drop off some papers that Ludovico had needed to see about the new shipment of goods. While there, I greeted Signora d'Invito and smiled broadly as Rachel was brought over to offer her pleasantries. Again, she met my gaze with more than a simple greeting, and I interpreted it in a very positive way for our relationship.

Signora d'Invito stood by watching the interaction, smiling knowingly but remaining quiet. While Ludovico reviewed the documents, Rachel was pushed forward gently by her mother and she offered me a cup of wine to enjoy while her father conducted his business. Signora d'Invito led me to a chair by the fire and Rachel returned with the wine. As she bent forward to present it to me, the low neckline of her dress revealed her womanly bounty, and I had to grip the cup firmly so as not to make a fool of myself.

Over the ensuing months, my business with Ludovico increased and the seed for such progress was
not lost on Rachel's parents. I was unaccustomed
to the subtleties of courting, but they were more
worldly. I suspect that Signora d'Invito knew the
truth right away, and if her husband also divined the
reason for my increased attention, he wouldn't object. His daughter's loveliness may have paved the
way for the d'Invito house to ally with the Trapensi
house, so an arranged marriage would benefit all
concerned.

In those visits, I secretly thanked the gods that
Rachel's music lessons had tapered off so that she
was more available to me and less available to Antonio. I knew that she had been moved from his studio,
but I didn't trust him in the company of the girls,
especially the one girl that I had watched grow up
and whom I now intended to wed.

* * *

In the recent weeks, the buzz about Vivaldi and Lalli
returned. With the two names caught in the same
conversation, I assumed that the gossip was once
again about the opera that had been banned. In-
terrogating those that I could reach, my suspicions

were justified, so I returned to the office and queried Dario about the news.

"He has convinced the elders of Venice to let him produce *Arsilda, Regina in Ponto,*" he replied.

"But you said it was about men engaging in unnatural love."

"Yes," he said with a chuckle, "but Lalli is a genius. He created a complicated love story where one character impersonates another, one is a woman and one is a man – or is it two of each? I can't remember – and so the reader of the story gets mixed up about the story. And Vivaldi charmed the old men of the city by retelling the story as a musical masterpiece, not a string of affairs. Meanwhile, your *maestro* reminded the men of the importance of his work to the city coffers, so they relented."

"Is it due to be produced here, then?" I asked.

"Yes, here. I suspect it will go forward in this very month."

And then he laughed again.

"I doubt that the younger people who attend this opera will be as confused about the trysts described as were the old men were."

* * *

It was apparent that Antonio's year back in Venice was a successful one. His new opera *Arsilda* was performed at the Teatro Sant'Angelo and the city fathers were left to wonder why the young audience was chortling throughout the production.

He wrote and arranged *L'incoronazione di Dario*, a story about a trio of pretenders to the throne of Persia, and their pursuit of the deceased king's daughter, Statira, whose hand in marriage would seal the suitor's claim to the crown.

"No, you're not the king of Persia," I had to remind my agent, although he and I shared an unfamiliar laugh over the subject.

Soon after, he produced *La Costanza Trionfante deglie Amori e degli Odi* at the Teatro San Moise here in Venice. It, too, was well received and I watched as Antonio's reputation grew from a violin virtuoso to a composer of great operas.

On the heels of these two masterpieces, word arrived in the city that his *La Stravanganza* was published in Amsterdam and dedicated to Victor Delfin, an adult student of Antonio's who lived here. The exact reasons for the dedication are not clear to me. Signor Delfin was a noted citizen of Venice and was familiar with Antonio in social circles, but these facts alone seem inconsequential when deciding to whom to dedicate a master work.

* * *

In deciding to query Antonio about this very point, I went to his apartment. The large home was subdivided and still occupied by his family members, but he had partitioned it so that a separate entrance was available for him to enter directly into his own salon by scaling a few steps on the outside of the building.

I did not approach that entrance but instead rapped on the door of the house itself and stood patiently while it swung open at the hand of Antonio's sister.

"He is not free at the moment, Signor Trapensi," she said, and I heard laughter from the east side of the building where Antonio's private apartment was. Without embarrassment, she told me that her brother was entertaining someone but that she would tell him that I had called.

The next day I visited his studio at the *Conservatorio*. He was between classes and so I watched as the small group of young girls collected their instruments and filed out of the room. When it was empty save for Antonio, I entered.

"How are you, Antonio?"

"Quite well, thank you, Domenico," he said, while continuing to straighten the papers on his desk. He raised his violin to waist level and plucked two of the strings without looking at me.

"And you?" he replied, still not looking in my direction.

"I am well. Thank you. I have been impressed with your latest productions. Do you have more such wonders to entertain your faithful Venetians with?"

"There will be more," he replied, but this time he looked at me.

"I am working on something grand, something that may take all of my time."

I had to admit to being dumbfounded by Antonio's output and how his reputation had soared in the past three years. I suppressed my envy for my own lost musical career but had since settled into the comfortable life of a successful merchant with a bright future.

As the next group of girls filed in for instruction, I turned to see Rachel passing through the door and taking her seat in front of Antonio's desk. My expression must have revealed my utter surprise; I was sure that she had ceased her violin lessons and embarked on her parents' current venture of finding a suitable husband. In fact, I was certain that I had made a successful play for Rachel's attention and visited her often. There was no hint during my visits to her home that she had resumed music instruction.

The girl nodded in my direction and smiled, a favor that calmed my nerves. But when she presented her violin and began to pull the bow across the strings, her attention went to Antonio and her placid expression took on the look of an impressionable girl blushing in the presence of her object of devotion.

The blood rose in my cheeks and I turned quickly to depart. Antonio didn't even notice my leaving, and I escaped the room without further embarrassment.

* * *

Some few days later I made another appearance at the d'Invito home and was received kindly. Rachel was there and she made gestures of interest as before and I returned to a feeling of hopefulness.

"Here is some wine for your thirst," she said. It was common in homes where the girl was being courted that the parents would receive the guest, but the girl would serve him.

"How are you today?" Rachel asked. It was also common that, once initial meetings were counted as past, the girl would be allowed to more often carry on conversations with the guest.

"I am well," I replied. "I see that you are learning violin at the master's knee." After the words came out, I wondered how they would be received. Did my question come across solely as interested curiosity, or complaint.

"Yes, but only for a few more lessons."

"And how is that?" I asked.

Ludovico entered the room at that point and walked toward his wife, seated at the other end of the table in the position of chaperone.

"He is a true talent," the man intoned, "and Rachel is quite taken with him."

"Quite taken with his talent," Signora d'Invito corrected. "His talent. Our daughter would like to be able to play the violin pleasantly for the husband that is chosen."

* * *

On my next visit to the d'Invito home, I saw a note tied to a flower at the threshold. The fold of the paper hid the contents of the message, but I could see the initials "A.V." on the corner that was exposed.

When Signora d'Invito opened the door to admit me, she saw the flower and attached note and scooped them up in one swing of her hand while pushing the door open for me.

That visit proceeded under the shadow of doubt, and I remained only long enough to convince Ludovico that I was an excellent suitor for his daughter. I was plotting to win her hand through her parents' choice, even if the young girl might have her own preoccupations.

May 1718
Venice

I carried on my courtship of Rachel for another year and then proposed marriage. During this period, she received interest from other men; I even caught sight of more than a single clandestine meeting or message from "A.V." But I was in a superior position to the other suitors and believed that I could win Rachel for myself despite the competition from younger – or more famous – others.

It was in the cold months of winter at the beginning of this year that I made a formal proposal. I was welcomed into the d'Invito home and presented Signora with a bouquet of flowers, a tribute nearly impossible to secure in mid-winter except by a man of significant wealth such as myself.

I presented Ludovico with a contract to award his company a sizable fortune, and he smiled grandly at the offer. We would now be in business together and I would hopefully be wed to his daughter to seal the enduring relationship.

Rachel was called from her room and I approached her with confidence. I had won the confidence and approval of her parents and I had no doubt that she would follow their decision. To please her and convince her of my sincerity, I presented Rachel with an ornately carved box with inlaid layers of various woods that curled and swooped across the surface in the image of a frozen set of roses. She raised the latch which held the box closed and peered inside.

I had purchased four gleaming items that were nested carefully in the velvet folds of the box. One was a necklace made of alternating sapphires and diamonds, another was an antique broach that I secured with great difficulty from a trading partner in the Far East. The third item was a bracelet that featured white gold fittings and a long trail of sparkling diamonds. The last of the four was a ring that held five diamonds in a cluster at the center, and thirteen smaller diamonds to decorate the band itself.

"There are eighteen diamonds in the ring, one for each of the years of your life, Rachel, with the five brightest and biggest in the center to represent the past five years since I fell in love with you.

Signora d'Invito smiled brightly at my description and my thoughtfulness; Ludovico smiled profitably about how his daughter had brought such success to his family.

"I have secured your parents' permission to marry you, but I want to know that you are willing."

Rachel thought for only a moment, then broke into a broad smile and thanked me for the gifts. Pausing only for another few seconds as if she might have forgotten something, she nodded her head and said, "yes."

* * *

We were married soon after that in a little ceremony in the chapel of the Madonna dell'Orto. A person of my stature and finances could have expected a grander celebration, but the d'Invito family was of more modest means and I was prepared to comply in order to gain the hand of the girl I had known since her birth.

Rachel appeared on that morning in a long white dress, her face hidden behind a gossamer veil and her arms cloaked in a white satin shawl. Her hands and fingers were similarly concealed, they within soft white cotton gloves, and her feet held in tiny white shoes with a row of buttons down the side. She was accompanied by her father down the aisle, her mother waiting patiently in the first pew of the church just in front of the elevated pulpit.

I was dressed formally and attended by Dario, at this point my 'next of kin,' although I didn't allow him to represent me in any way other than by his attendance.

There were only about one hundred guests, but even that number was achieved only when I volunteered to host the *festa* that was to come after the ceremony. I recall the priest intoning the blessing and vows, but I have little memory even now so soon afterward of what was said. I was proud to be marrying such a beautiful girl and my focus was on her, not the proceedings. When I glanced at Rachel, I could see little of her face although she seemed in rapt attention to the words of the celebrant.

When we were dismissed from the church, we paraded down the Calle Piave and crossed the bridge that brought the wedding party to a large ristorante that I had reserved for us on the Fondamenta de la Sensa. There, toasts were given to the bride and to me, and I stood to provide the oration that was customary for the groom.

"It is with great pleasure and a distinct honor that we unite the families of Trapensi and d'Invito on this day," I began. I knew that family reputation was of paramount concern in marriages in Venetian culture, so I introduced that first.

"And I am pleased and also honored to take Rachel d'Invito as my wife." The initial comment drew light applause, and the second brought nodding heads and a repeat of the respectful applause.

I thought that I should say more but I was not a man of words and quickly came to a shortage of things to say. So, I raised my cup of wine and sipped from it, followed by others in the room, and then I sat down.

April 1719
Mantua

The Trapensi business was proceeding as planned, with increases in imports and exports, and the revenues were increasing apace. I would claim credit for the success, at least in public, but recoiled from raising it in the presence of Dario, who might think that each accomplishment chronicled in the Trapensi ledger was his.

My father stayed engaged, too, as if to deprive me of the titular head of the business. In recent months he had taken to his bed and remained there for most hours of the day, taking his meals while propped up on pillows and scouring Dario's registers for any items of interest. His meals were brought to him in the apartment above the office which he occupied now nearly full time, and his irascibility increased as the months went by, so much so that I once heard the household staff drawing lots to see who would be required to bring Signor Trapensi his tray in the evening.

I was not surprised on one recent afternoon when my father asked for me to visit with him. He was more than ever focused on the family business. I couldn't decide whether this fervor was borne of his lack of faith in my abilities or a natural artifact of a man's mind as he nears death. Although it seemed to me that he passed more responsibilities on to me, his only surviving son, rather than to Dario – his chosen agent – at this time of passage, and I took solace in that thought.

"I want you to go to Mantua and introduce yourself to Adolfo Gagliardo," he said. "He represents a significant market for us in that area of Italy, and I want you to come to know him well."

I knew the man's name. It appeared quite often in the Trapensi books; in fact, I believe that I had already met him, but it was some time ago and neither he nor I would recall the occasion.

"He is prepared to sell off a large share of his import business," my father explained. "He's old and has no one to give it to," and I thought I heard a pause in my father's voice. Was it because he had me to pass on the family business, unlike this poor old Gagliardo fellow?

"You will meet with him," my father said. He never requested or inquired; he only gave instructions. "I have already driven a bargain; it is only for you to finish it."

I made arrangements to depart two days later, instructing Dario and his assistants to load my trunk onto the carriage after the morning meal. It would be a two-day journey and I hoped to reach a comfortable inn by nightfall of the first day and leave ample time to reach Mantua on the following day before dark.

"Sire," offered the liveryman, "do you know that your countryman, Antonio Vivaldi, is in Mantua of this day?"

I did not, and told the man so, but didn't otherwise admit to any interest in the subject. I had heard that Antonio was abroad again and that he would be performing in the hinterland of Venice. I didn't know that Mantua was his destination but would not be surprised if he was in that place.

Upon arriving in Mantua, I was settled quickly into a formidable house owned by the widow of a former city councilman. The accommodations were fine and I appreciated the location near the river and the business center of Mantua. Arriving late in the evening, I took my supper in my room and retired soon after the sunset.

Business was conducted on the following day as I met with Signor Gagliardo just after the midday meal. As stated, my father had already made all the arrangements; I was there simply to sign for the Trapensi family. It was an impressive sale. We got most of Gagliardo's clients and some of his warehouse stock. He received only employment guarantees for his principal men, since he had no heirs to pass the profits on to, and a promise that a statue would be erected in his honor in the main piazza of Mantua after his passing.

I happened to come across the *maestro* Antonio on my walk back to lodgings that afternoon.

"Ah, Domenico," he said with high greetings. "I heard that you were in Mantua."

"Yes, Antonio. I am conducting business here," I replied.

"And so am I," he said, waving his hand in the direction of a large, ornately decorated façade of the theatre across the way. "I am performing a new piece here, tonight in fact. Will you come?"

The Teatro Arciducale was Mantua's pearl of architecture. The high walls and arched windows dominated the piazza and the lanterns lit at its entrance dominated the dark corners of the square. I had heard that Antonio had written an opera, *Tito Manlio* I recalled, and that the soprano that he discovered to perform in it delivered such magic as to rob even Antonio of the central credit for the performance.

"Yes, I will come," I said.

"Good. I will introduce you to Anna," he said, as if this female *virtuosa* was his to show off.

That evening, I arrived at the theatre and was greeted at the door by a man that I did not know. He introduced himself as a friend of Antonio Vivaldi and he escorted me to a seat in a private box just off stage left, "the preferred angle for viewing" he said.

Anna Tessieri Girò was just as amazing as I had heard. Her voice was as gentle as an angel's but carried the force of an entire host of them. At the end of the performance, Antonio joined her onstage and bowed with her, and the impression he gave was that they shared the performance and the accolades showered down upon them.

On the following evening, I was invited to dine with Antonio and several of his entourage, which included Anna and her sister, Paolina, and I got the distinct impression that Antonio was involved with both of the women. He had always flirted with the pretty young girls and more seriously wooed the more mature older women, but the attention he showed Anna was of a special nature. He was attentive to Paolina also, and one might have wondered about his relations with both women at a time, but even she – Paolina – was secondary to the favor he showed to the young soprano.

* * *

In the months since I saw Antonio in Mantua, I heard many stories of his travels and his life, and Anna always seemed to be included in the telling. I did not envy him his amorous adventures with the young singer, in fact I felt that this might represent a turn in his life. He had a reputation with women and finding someone who might equal him in talent encouraged me to think that he would settle down and leave the ladies of Venice alone. I thought especially of Rachel when this thought occurred to me, even though I had not seen any of his missives with "A.V." initialed on them lately.

August 1721
Venice and Milan

I had hoped by this time that Rachel would have given me children to fill the household, but it was not to be. I continued with my work at the Trapensi office – my father had passed away in the previous winter – and she remained to manage the affairs of the home.

I traveled a bit more after my father's passing. He had not been on the road very much in the preceding years, and I needed to re-establish contacts that he had nurtured. Milan was a frequent posting for me since so much of the trade in Italy found itself in the business centers of that city, and I had arranged an apartment for myself to come to whenever I would visit.

It was in the latter part of August in this year that I went to Milan and found that Antonio had just arrived to compose and perform an opera. He titled it *La Silvia* and relied on Enrico Bissari for the lyrics. The venue was the Teatro Regio Ducale and the opera achieved the high acclaim that Antonio had grown accustomed to. I did not see him on my own; I was too busy for social engagements. But I heard that he traveled with a young woman who fit the description of Anna Girò. The opera was performed for only a few evenings, and I remained in Milan for two weeks beyond that.

A note was left on my desk at the apartment. It was from Antonio. He expressed pleasure that I was in the city but disappointment that we did not get together while time allowed. "I am off to Venice," he signed the note, "and I hope to see you upon your return."

I stayed a while longer in Milan on business, and when I returned from Milan, I was greeted with smiles and tenderness from Rachel. But I was put on suspicion by the maid, Manola. She avoided my gaze and gave only short replies to my questions. When Rachel was absent at the market, I regarded her personal possessions in the room that was hers, and found a scrap of paper with "*Sempre, A.V.*" – "Always, A.V." – scribbled across it. I detected a faint aroma of the perfume that Rachel wore when we went about the town. I returned the scrap to folds of the blouse in which I had found it.

January 1722
Venice and Milan

Another year passed and still no children to inherit the business that Trapensi had built. I was often traveling between cities and increasing the market yield of our imports, and left Rachel behind in the care of Manola, our man servant who managed the small craft used to navigate the canals of Venice, and Dario who was still the most able accountant.

I passed through Milan and was told that Antonio Vivaldi had just visited there, only a short time, but long enough to present a new opera, *L'adorazione delli Tre Re Magi al Bambino Gesù* – Adoration of the Three Kings for the Baby Jesus. It was received with great applause but remained on people's minds only a short time. By now, Antonio was producing operas and other works with such great speed that one masterpiece nearly stumbled onto the one before.

When I returned to Venice, more quickly than I had on past trips, I found that Rachel was visiting her parents. She had grown lonely during my absence, or so Manola reported, and she spent the days with her mother to recount her young life – she was still only twenty-two years of age and I a mature forty-four – and passed her time in the comfort of her mother's care.

With her absence from our home, I looked through her things in the bedroom across from mine and found little to arouse suspicion. Until I noticed a slip of paper pushed under the cushion of her bed. A note scribbled in the same hand simply said, "A.V."

I also heard that Antonio had returned from Milan to Venice for one week before departing for an assignment in Roma. When I questioned Manola, she had little to say, and Dario was curt and uninformative as usual.

I called on the d'Invito household and was greeted kindly by Signora d'Invito. Hearing my voice, Rachel emerged from another room and rushed to me for an embrace. Her smile was radiant, as was her voice and expression. It removed all doubt from my mind and I smiled in return.

April 1725
Venice

The years of early marriage passed quickly. I became more absorbed in the Trapensi business, Rachel's time was spent managing our home and maintaining contacts with the social world that she had grown up in and to which she had been introduced by my world of business.

We still had no children owing mostly to God's choice, although my trips abroad increased and Rachel's reception upon my return cooled some over time. I continued to do my part to create a new generation of Trapensis, but was discouraged by Rachel's failure to return to me each fortnight with the long-awaited news.

Venice also continued to develop as a center for art and music. Great masters from the surrounding area came our city, some drawn by the fame of local composers like Vivaldi, some in search of new opportunities in a venue that welcomed performances of this nature.

These new arrivals also brought innovation to the music of Venice. Something called sympathetic strings was introduced to the instruments long revered in palaces of music. As well as I could tell, it involved the pairing of minor strings on such things as the violin and cello to pick up additional vibrations and tonal notes and underscore the primary note struck on the main string. I heard some of these instruments being played but didn't pay very much attention until I returned to the *Conservatorio* on my usual inspection visit.

Since marrying Rachel, I terminated her music lessons which removed her from the school and, therefore, from direct contact with Antonio. I expected that marriage itself, and my directive to avoid such contacts would be enough, but I continued to find odd clues to indicate that A.V. was still pestering my wife. I planned to confront Antonio directly. I recognized his reputation with women and his apparently irresistible craving for the young and unreachable females, but I would not tolerate my spouse being set in his sights.

Upon visiting the *Conservatorio*, I made straight away for his studio. He was entertaining a trio of young girls, all pretty and precocious, who had to stifle the giggles that accompanied the flirtatious behavior of youth. As for himself, Antonio remained barely aloof, but touched each girl in turn on the shoulder – or at times lower on the skin that was exposed – and kept them working on their instruments despite the girls' alternative reasons for being with the *maestro* in this room. At forty-seven years, Antonio was three times the age of these young girls, but they still swooned at his touch.

"Perhaps you should find someone to marry," I said when the girls had completed their lesson and departed. "You could father a great musician to carry on your legend, as your father has done for you."

My suggestion met with no recognition from Antonio. But then he brightened and turned to me face on.

"Yes, Domenico. It is good for a man to carry on his line through marriage."

He didn't say anything more on that, but I was left with the feeling that he was talking about me, not himself.

"Rachel and I are very happy together," I continued, changing the topic slightly. "And we have plans to continue the Trapensi line. Perhaps you should visit us sometime?"

As soon as I tossed out the casual invitation, I wondered what I was doing. Was it my subconscious self trying to smoke out some small detail of truth, or to elicit an unintentional gesture or expression from Antonio that would be his undoing.

"Yes, that would be nice," he replied lamely. Then he finished packing his instrument and other implements of music and turned to go.

"Yes, I should do that. It would be good to see Rachel again," he said before turning toward the door.

May 1725
Venice and Amsterdam

While he flitted about the countryside and crafted new operas for the masses, Antonio was spending months on one particular invention. I had no insight into his work at this point, so relied on rumors and comments made in public spaces to track his work.

I had also made the decision to ignore the musician's progress. He had succeeded, it was true, in the field that I once desired. Although since those early days of frivolous youth, I had matured and realized that the business of the market was the truest pursuit, and one that the Trapensi family excelled at. So, I had no use of, nor time for, his music.

But most of Venice was still enthralled by him including, apparently, my wife. Rachel was not permitted to travel out by herself, but when my interest in music flagged, she enlisted the support of her mother, a matronly woman whom all would agree was a safe escort. Rachel attended small concerts but also took an interest in the grander productions that Venice had become known for. With Antonio traveling so much, he was seldom the center of attention at these productions, but when he was present in the city, his attendance at the event sparked additional interest on her part.

On one particular evening, I delivered Rachel into her mother's care at their family home. They were to dine together and proceed to the concert hall and I was going to attend to business. But after another hour or so, one of my ships docked with cargo from Asia and brought along a surprise visitor. It was Vittorio Giglio, the son of my father's business associate from Rimini and the only man in my generation of business that I delighted in seeing. He appeared unannounced at the door of my office on the quay and let himself in before the doorman could respond.

"It's time!" he announced gaily. I couldn't comprehend his salutation and was confused at first.

"You're always here at the office," he said rather too loud for my comfort. "You never play about this wonderful city!"

By then, I had caught onto his jest, because most people believed I put in too little time to support the import business, relying almost totally on Dario. Vittorio was upbraiding me for that in a reverse form, and I shook my head as he did so.

"It's time. We should go out," he continued.

"Of course," I replied. "We should."

As I gathered my hat and light evening coat, Vittorio held out a hand to stop me.

"But not so fast. It is not even sundown. I will return to the ship, collect my wife – oh, yes! she accompanied me this time – and we will meet later at Le Bon Vignoble, that little place you said your friend Filipe brags about.

"I hadn't counted on your wife being here. Rachel is with her mother and they will be attending the concert tonight."

"Not tonight. Tonight, we will drink wine and our wives will prattle on about children."

As quickly as he said it, Vittorio halted, and cast his eyes down.

"*Mi dispiace, amico.*" – I'm sorry my friend – "I didn't mean that the way it sounded. Attempting to recover, Vittorio added, "Sara needs someone other than me to talk to about the little *bambini*, and I'm sure Rachel is preparing to bring her brood into the world too."

I let the moment pass and promised to collect Rachel and meet Vittorio and Sara at the restaurant later.

After seeing my friend out the door, I turned my attention to closing up the books in the office and then departed for the d'Invito house. When the door opened, Signora d'Invito was standing there with a look of surprise on her face.

"Won't you come in, sir?" she said. I entered through the doorway and observed that Rachel was sitting at the table with her father, Ludovico, and her little sister. The meal was nearly completed, and so the signora apologized to me and then left the room to gather some small victuals for me.

"No. Thank you," I said to delay her. "We will be joining friends tonight for supper."

"But I have already eaten," Rachel said, pointing to her plate, then added, "We supped early so that we could go to the concert in a bit."

Rachel had dressed for the occasion before leaving our house, but I could see that her mother had not yet donned her evening clothes.

"Well, so I see. But Vittorio and his wife Sara appeared without notice, and I said that we would meet them this evening."

Seeing Rachel's look of delay – or was it disappointment? – I assured her that she would not have to join in the entire meal; that I would explain that she had given up the concert to be with us.

"Perhaps," I suggested, "if Signora d'Invito does not mind, perhaps you could entice Sara to join you for the concert tonight."

Signora d'Invito seemed unmoved by this decision and I wondered again about why she had not prepared herself for the evening out.

"I do not know her very well, though," Rachel said. "I mean, we could dine together, but I don't even know if she cares for music."

"We shall see," I responded.

I sent word to the ship about the possible plans, adding for Vittorio's consideration that we would be allowed to enjoy the wine better if alone, and received word back that Sara would accompany Rachel to the concert.

We returned to our home so that I could attend to some few small matters. Rachel lingered by the door as I gave Manola instructions about the time of our return, and we started out. We would meet Vittorio and his wife at Le Bon Vignoble and enjoy a small meal, the women would proceed to the concert hall, and Vittorio and I would find a suitable café to continue our own private conversation.

Over the brief time that we dined, Rachel picked at her food and seemed listless. She excused herself once to attend to private matters and Sara followed her out into the square.

"I need some air," my wife said, but I hadn't noticed any concerns for health up until that moment.

"Maybe, just maybe..." Vittorio began, with a poorly hidden smile of anticipation on his face.

I ignored his gesture. I knew nothing about women's medical matters, but I knew that months of celibacy were not likely to produce babies.

Looking through the crowded tables, I could see the women standing on the portico just outside the door. Then Sara returned to our table.

"Poor Rachel is discomfited. I am going to escort her to her home and then return to our berth on the ship. She'll be more comfortable in bed this evening."

"But you can't wander about the city," Vittorio protested.

"Rachel already offered to have Manola escort me back to the ship." Of course, the need for Manola to return alone along the city streets didn't occur to any of us.

My wife's condition worried me, but Sara assured me that it was nothing terrible. Just a womanly thing. She smiled and patted my arm, then bade Vittorio and me a happy evening and returned to Rachel, together walking into the dark night.

Vittorio and I did not avail ourselves of the unused Trapensi box at the concert hall that evening. "I plan to drink!" he said as his preferred alternative. We ordered more food and wine and, when the supper was over, we remained at the table for another bottle of wine.

* * *

The next morning while walking to my office, I over-heard many reports of the performance the evening before. It was Antonio's newest production, *Le Quat-tro Stagioni,* styled some said after the four seasons of the year around Mantua. I remembered that the woman Anna Girò was from Mantua, the one Antonio was rumored to have been in love with, and I wondered – or should I say, hoped – that she was the inspiration for the new production.

In any case, those who had attended the concert were rapturous in their praise of the new work. Comparing it plainly to the seasons themselves, the descriptions talked of the serenity of spring, the oppressiveness of summer, and the quiet strength of winter. These were words used to describe the various movements of the concert themselves, not the seasons that inspired Antonio, but the people were emphatic about the "utter presence" of each season

– as one observer was heard to say – in the music composition itself.

Very soon, *Le Quattro Stagioni* drew the attention of visitors to Venice and seats in the theatre became quite scarce. I had our private box, but I didn't bother to attend Antonio's second or third production of the piece, until two weeks later when Rachel insisted that we go.

The program said that the four movements of that composition would dominate the evening, but that eight other violin concertos would be performed first. All were attributed to Antonio Vivaldi.

We took our seats in the box and made ourselves comfortable while waiting for the rest of the concert goers to find their seats in the lower tiers. I told Rachel how lovely she looked that evening, and she smiled kindly at me, and patted my hand in thanks. Our box was enclosed by tapestries on the sides and a drape in front that was folded back to the edges and tied with a soft, braided rope. The attendant entered the box from behind us to extinguish the candles in the chandelier above our heads, and that signaled that the performance was about to begin.

Despite my long years of dwindling interest in the violin, and music generally, I was inordinately impressed by the performance that Antonio delivered that evening. It wasn't immediately obvious to me whether it was his composition – truly, *Le Quattro Stagioni* was the best I had ever heard from Vivaldi – or his performance of it. The assembled crowd agreed with my assessment. As the last note of *L'Inverno* – winter – drifted up into the cushioned quadrants of the vaulted ceiling, the mass of people rose in thunderous applause.

I did not stand; such behavior would not fit my station. But I looked at Rachel to gauge her impression. She had not stood either, but a look of wonder and utter enchantment was upon her. She stared at Antonio as he absorbed the applause and when I glanced at her again, even the dim light of our box could not hide the light blush on her cheeks.

As the crowd below us began to clear, Rachel stood and leaned forward on the railing of our box. Antonio returned to the edge of the stage to wave at the departing crowd and threw a glance in our direction.

* * *

In a very short time, the success of *Le Quattro Stagioni* became common knowledge. Reports were received from faroff cities vying for Antonio to visit and present it there, although to date no one other than Venetians had heard it performed. It wasn't until a publisher named Michel-Charles Le Cène decided to publish the complete work in Amsterdam that this production became commonly known to the public. Taken together, Le Cène's booklet was labeled as *Il Cimento dell'Armonia e dell'Inventione* – The Contest between Harmony and Invention – and it was regarded as one of Antonio's most complex and cerebral productions.

The success of *Le Quattro Stagioni* also drew the attention of Count Wenzel von Morzin, a nobleman in Roma, who sponsored Antonio during a long-term correspondence that benefited both men. Antonio received the monetary support of a man who could afford him, and von Morzin basked in the reflected glory as the benefactor of a famous musician and composer.

May 1730
Venice and Trieste

As Antonio's reputation continued to grow, so did his absences from Venice. He traveled to Roma often and to Mantua – no doubt to see Anna Girò – and returned to our city periodically. It was reported that he was completing some new work and desired the comfort of his own private apartment or the familiar surroundings of his studio at the *Conservatorio*.

As for me, Rachel and I had grown accustomed to each other and the flame of our marriage dimmed. I still loved her and she showed all the love I would expect from a wife, but my travels and her inability to produce a child altered our relationship in ways that I didn't expect.

Often, when I arrived home from a trip and Manola would open the door for me to enter, my first sight would be of Rachel sitting on the dais just below the window. She was an excellent seamstress and, although we could afford to have all our clothing made by the women in town, Rachel preferred to busy herself with this endeavor. She seemed relaxed when engaged in that activity, but always set it aside quickly when I came through the door, eagerly embracing me and ushering met to the hearth to join her in conversation.

"What was it like?" she would ask about the city that I had just come from. I would answer her questions and take comfort in her interest in my affairs. Manola knew the routine, too, and she would come forward in a few minutes with wine and food for me. I always enjoyed this time, returning to the warmth of my home and the attentions of my wife, even if the ardor of young love had escaped me. Rachel was still young, of course, not quite thirty yet, but by this time I was fifty-two years old and desiring the routine of home life and office more than the traveling that the business required of me.

I humored Rachel's love of music and we attended the opera at times when I was home. I knew that she afforded herself of our box in the concert hall in my absences, always accompanied by someone – usually her mother – and I was not going to restrain the interest she had. Like me, she had given up playing the violin, although she seemed more affected by the loss than I was. She certainly did not take lessons any more, and I hoped that this ensured her distance from Antonio.

"What did you see?" I would ask her about her trips to the concert hall. It was a fond question although it might have seemed like prying. Rachel did not usually mention a work by Antonio, as if she was not in the audience when his compositions were performed, but I noticed that Manola would look away when I asked that question. I interpreted it as the maid's attempt to avoid being part of a half-truth.

I still saw Filipe when he burst into town and I had to sit quietly as he expounded on his travels. He was about my age but seemed to have more energy; perhaps it was my bad leg that had taken a toll on my ability to travel. And he would prattle on about news of Antonio from abroad.

"The report is that he has the attention of the Emperor," he said, but Filipe's report was not true. Such rumors abounded, but we knew that this one was an exaggeration.

"He was also grandly received in Prague earlier this year, performing a new opera," he continued. "Umm, what is the name of that thing?"

"*Farnace*," I replied. Filipe was a worldly traveler, but he seemed to only grasp a thin veneer of everything around him. His stories of the cities tended to focus on women and café life; anecdotes from the road were flighty; and his reports of Antonio, all glowing, lacked basic information, for example the name of the opera that Antonio had just composed. *Farnace* was Vivaldi's rewrite of an earlier opera, a work that was performed at our very own Teatro Sant'Angelo, so I would already know of it and wasn't surprised when Filipe confused the location of its performance.

"Do you see him often?" Filipe asked.

"Not very, but Rachel does." The last words slipped off my tongue without my intention to say them. I had come to assume that it was true, and that she was in attendance when his works were performed, but I harbored dark thoughts about my wife visiting Antonio at other times. When I had talked around the subject with her, I noticed that Manola always removed herself from the room. I also noticed that Rachel made careful choice of her words in those conversations.

"She does, huh?" replied Filipe with a smile that he quickly swept from his face. Talk of a man's wife seeing someone else, particularly someone who was famous, was not the type of subject that should be pursued for long.

"Well," he added when he composed himself, "she is lucky to have you and the Trapensi quarters at the concert hall so that she can arrive and leave without facing the commoners in the pit."

* * *

I maintained a casual relationship with Antonio. Knowing him since our birth in the same year and growing up among the favored gentlemen of Venice made it nearly impossible to avoid contact, although Rachel's evasion of my questions and occasional references to A.V. in my home – indiscrete code between Manola and my wife – suggested he was imperiling the sanctity of my marriage.

While touring *L'Ospedale* and the *Conservatorio* one afternoon, I found myself unconsciously going toward his studio. A lesson was in progress but when it ended Antonio invited me in with a ready smile.

"How are you, Domenico? I trust that the Trapensi business is flourishing still?"

"Yes, it is." His warmth and carefree greeting rankled me. I had good reason to suspect him of adding my wife to his harem of female admirers, yet his humor seemed to pay no heed to that which he was doing to me.

"Are you writing something?" I said, pushing papers back and forth on his desk, as if searching for something.

"I am always writing," he replied, but then he stopped and looked down at the floor. He had a vacant stare that was out of character with the joyful way he had received me. I had heard that he was teaching more students and selling some of his works for others to perform, and that this new approach to income was due to the steady decline of his popularity. Certainly, the name Antonio Vivaldi drew great comment in all civilized societies still, but he had been producing music for thirty years and promoters knew the importance of hiring new talent.

Antonio kept his solemn gaze for a moment but awoke from it and regained his gay demeanor. If a decline in his fortune was the reason for his contemplation, he seemed able to erase it from the moment.

July 1732
Venice and Prague

Antonio's travels had put him into contact with sponsors and producers of music in many other cities. So, as the charm of newness began to recede among his Venetian followers, he pursued opportunities abroad. He resurrected some of his earlier works, those that had not been performed outside our city, and delivered them elsewhere to a new round of applause.

Artabano Re dei Parti is an example of this. I heard from travelers and business associates that he had performed that opera in Prague during this year and it was well received. I also heard tattles about his personal affairs, including the attention that Antonio got from the women of Prague. My strength might be diminishing, but his hunger had apparently not.

Which put me in mind of my wife again. If she were somehow involved with Antonio I would cast her out of my house. But that couldn't be! She could not have stooped to infelicitous behavior.

And, for that matter, I could not cast her out. I loved her and knew that she loved me. If I did not serve in the full role of husband as she might have expected, that would be my failure, for which I could not hold her responsible.

But I would hold Antonio responsible for attracting her attention.

February 1736
Venice

His flirtation with other cities was taking its toll on Antonio and, as the years piled on, he became more likely to remain in Venice, especially during the difficult travel months of winter. And this season had been particularly rainy and cold, conditions which I experienced as pain in my joints and a more listless-than-usual left leg.

The cafés were empty and people traversed the streets and little bridges of the city with shoulders hunched against the wind, wrapped in shawls and rough woolen coats to keep the chill air at bay, and under hats that were often sent flying by a sudden and unexpected gust of wind.

Rachel remained at home much of the time. Her mother had passed away at the dawn of this winter and her father had removed himself from active work, leaving the business he had formed to his son, Brie. Without a maternal figure to accompany her on evenings out – and I displaying greater reluctance to socialize – my wife found herself with more idle time to be spent with Manola in our home.

Rachel seemed to have taken on the lassitude of the season. She continued with her sewing and would occasionally accompany Manola into the city for the necessaries of life, but when she spoke to me it seemed as if coming from the bottom of a well, in a small voice without amplitude. She smiled less often, although she still tried to grace me with that little pleasure at times. She also ate less and the hollowing of her cheeks gave away her loss of weight.

The one thing that still buoyed Rachel's spirit was music. Without her mother as chaperone, she enlisted Manola's accompaniment and together they attended the opera and other music festivities when they were available. I accompanied her on some but noticed that Rachel's interest was more mixed when I was her companion.

By this time, we had forgotten about the prospects of children. They had not come of their own accord and Rachel and I did little on our part to promote the possibility. A thin veneer of love remained; I was respectful and Rachel was dutiful, but that sort of love does not always lend itself to romance.

There was a short-lived burst of warmer weather, when the air was clear and the sun shone in the sky, but that brief respite from the damp season disappeared as quickly as it came. And Rachel's mood was a mirror image of that dispiriting curve in the elements. In that brief respite with blue skies and a warm sun, she brightened and dragged Manola along on a visit to the *Conservatorio*.

"I'm going to listen to the music," she said.

"But there is no concert," I reminded her.

"No matter," was her response. "It is the middle of the afternoon and there would be no concert. But I want music," she continued, but added sorrowfully, "and I cannot play the violin anymore so I have to listen to someone who can."

I worried as I saw them out the door, worrying that Rachel's real reason for going to *L'Ospedale's Conservatorio* was to see Antonio – although I had to admit that I didn't even know if he was still teaching there. And I worried that my wife's frail state might challenge her health if the afternoon sunshine declined and she didn't come home before the colder air of evening returned.

Instead of passing my time at the office, I decided to remain at home, prepared for Rachel's return whenever it would occur. As I feared, the women didn't come through the door until far past sunset and, although the air was still barely pleasant, the fading heat of the sun allowed a chill breeze to blow through the door as they entered.

Rachel was in a better mood and sat down in her usual chair. She began to talk about the music and the performers they had witnessed that afternoon, but her words were cast out into the room without addressing anyone in particular, certainly not me. Manola stood by watching her and noticed the same thing, although the maid's concern for my wife was of a different sort than my own. I was Rachel's husband but I understood little of what motivated a woman, and nothing at all about their feelings. Manola stood by Rachel with a hand on her shoulder, offering a human touch of support that would not have occurred to me.

At one point Rachel mentioned Antonio's name. It was the first I had heard her speak of him for many months and it confirmed to me that he was still about the city. In fact, it seemed from her rambling narrative that he was at the *Conservatorio* that very day.

"It was wonderful," Rachel said to the vacant space in front of her. "Wonderful."

After a while, Manola helped Rachel into bed, and promised to bring her some soup and little bites to eat shortly. The maid returned to the main room in our house where I still sat staring into the fireplace. Without bothering to converse with me, Manola passed through the room and began preparation of food. She served mine on a tray and then swept back into the kitchen to retrieve Rachel's portion.

Manola carried my wife's tray into the bedroom but soon returned with it.

"The lady is asleep," she reported to me, in a most dutiful tone.

My hunger was blunted by the events of the day but I dawdled long enough over the supper to make a good show of eating it.

Manola retired for the night while I still sat before the fireplace. The food was still on the tray and I declined her offer to remove it.

"I'll finish it," I said. "So let it be."

After a long time – I lost track of the evening – I retired to my bed and slept fitfully that night. Rachel's condition worried me, but so did the brightening of her spirit at the mention of Antonio's name.

* * *

Several days later the cold weather had settled in all through the city and people's moods worsened with it. As for Rachel, she became despondent with the departure of the sunny weather and sometimes asked Manola about music, in a voice that seemed devoid of life.

"Yes," the maid would reply. "It was wonderful. Would you like to hear more of it?"

"Oh, yes," my wife would say, but then her head would sink back down onto the pillow and she would drift off into sleep.

"How is the lady?" Dario asked me when I arrived at the office later that same day.

"She is well. But like most Venetians in this terrible weather, she is afflicted by the cold."

I didn't know how much Dario understood about my life at home; I knew that Manola never came to the office so they would have no opportunity to talk. But his questions combined compassion for Rachel with a level of inquisitiveness that made me wonder about his intent.

When I completed my review of the books that Dario presented, I did something unusual for me – I went down to the docks. I had traditionally kept a distance from the ships themselves, preferring my perch in the office window above them, but wandered down among the dock workers and ship loaders along the water as they moved the crates of goods onto and off of the vessels. The weather was still inclement and I had to pull the collar up on my coat against the chill air, but instead of burying my chin in my chest I kept my head up and eyes peering keenly at the operations going on before me.

The ship's manifest that I had just read detailed all the materials that we had imported and also spoke of how they would be distributed about the city. I knew these facts from the books, but had never inspected what this meant on the docks. Now, standing among the piles of cargo, I could see that the numbers etched in the book for each type of import were repeated on the crates themselves, with circles around those that accompanied additional crates. I assumed from this that the uncircled numbers meant that the box was meant to stand alone and asked a dockhand if this was true.

"Yes, sire. This is the way we keep and separate the cargo for delivery." He certainly recognized me but seemed a little surprised that I had to ask for clarification of a matter that he considered so obvious in his worklife.

There were pulleys with great wooden tackles to lift the boxes, and strong men who worked in light shirts to vent the heat that their bodies generated by the effort. There were wagons and horses to pull the boxes and other, younger men and boys to help direct the crates lifted by the pulleys, placing the cargo onto the wagons for delivery.

I stayed long enough to notice how the great hulk of the ship changed over the time of its emptying. When I first came down to the waterside, the vessel was heavy with cargo and weighed deeply in the water, the solid thud of its hull knocking against the broad wood beams of the dock. As the cargo was lifted from its hold, the weight of the ship lessened and it rose in the water until I could see the barnacled beams of its lower hull appear above the surface. Then, the sound made by the hull became a more hollow thunk as it bounded back and forth in the light waves.

Shouts from the deckhands were constant throughout the operation, while the captain stood quiet and motionless on the deck, content to supervise the operation but only intervening with a command when it seemed his ship was being mishandled.

In time, the piles of cargo stacked on the dock were gone, dispatched to the wagons that were dispatched into the city. The sounds of work subsided and the captain disappeared from view, and I was left nearly alone on the quay. I turned toward the city myself and began the short walk over the cobblestones and little bridges to the home that I occupied with Rachel.

* * *

Manola admitted me to our house and advised me in a whispered voice that "my lady is sleeping." It was something that Rachel did much of the time these days and I worried then, as I had worried for weeks, about the portent of that.

But Rachel didn't tell me that there was also a doctor in the house, a Maximian Aurelio whom I knew from our social circle of businessmen and the elders of Venice. He emerged from Rachel's room and approached me still standing with my coat and scarf.

"Signor Trapensi," he began in a soft voice that conveyed sympathy, "Signora Trapensi is not well. She is afflicted by a fever," he said, but then he lowered his voice, "but I have been speaking with her for some weeks now…"

This was not something I knew about, and I shot an angry look at Manola for hiding this fact from me.

"…and I believe she may be suffering from more than a fever."

"What do you mean by that?" I asked. My voice had risen a bit and I worked to control it. Whatever news the doctor had for me would not benefit from a confrontation.

"She asks questions for which there are no answers, and talks of music as if she is singing the notes. She tells me stories of long ago, when she was a young girl, and of the violin. When I ask her about you, she says, 'oh, yes, Signor Trapensi' as if she is only lightly acquainted with you."

"And what else?"

"She asks if I will stay to hear her play the violin, but Manola signals me at these moments that there is no violin in the house."

"My lady has not played the violin for many years," Manola chimed in.

"I think she needs observation," Aurelio suggested.

"And you are doing so," I replied.

"Yes, but more than that."

"What do you mean?"

The doctor looked at Manola and then back at me.

"You are very kind to the signora," he said to me and then, indicating the maid, added, "and she is very attentive. But Signora Trapensi is frail. And she does not often know the day, or the time of day."

His continued narrative on Rachel's condition did not answer my question about observation.

"She should be in *L'Ospedale*," he said finally. "To be watched and cared for."

I was surprised by the revelation. I knew that Rachel had been in poor spirits of late, and that her youthful vigor had left her, but I thought of this as a condition of the winter, a condition that would dissipate with the coming of the spring. I told the doctor this.

"Yes, I see," he replied. "But her condition began last year, in the summertime."

I looked at Manola who looked away from my gaze.

"What would you do for her?" I asked.

The doctor's explanation included references to certain ointments, specific ways of eating, and control of moods with light and temperature. Most of it left me confused, and my attention waned in the telling of it.

"When?" I asked, and with that single word I realized that I had succumbed to the notion that Rachel would be taken from me and possibly never be returned.

"Right away, I would suggest. But it is up to you."

I turned away from the doctor, letting my scarf drop onto the chair beside me, and considered my next words.

"Will she be better?"

"We can make sure she is comfortable."

"And what does that mean?"

Doctor Aurelio didn't attempt a response to that question. I looked at Manola once again and she stared right back at me.

"Please prepare the signora's things," I said to her. "We will accompany her to *L'Ospedale*."

"That would not be the best way," the doctor interjected, but I looked at him with surprise.

"We have found that a husband leaving a woman at the door of *L'Ospedale* leaves a profound, and negative memory that she must then shake. I have already called for a carriage. We will transport Signora Trapensi ourselves."

He turned to Manola then, repeated my instructions to gather Rachel's things, and left the house.

* * *

Later that evening, with Rachel gone and Manola preparing my evening meal, I sat by the fireplace and stared into the flames. I did not know what my next actions would be, or what the coming days and weeks had in store for me.

I ate in silence and then Manola collected the tray. After cleaning up, she approached me with a question that I hadn't heard in the years since she came into my employment.

"Shall I return to my family, sir?"

Manola had lived with us for a very long time, spending long hours and even some nights tending to our household and to my wife. I knew she had a husband and children, but it had never occurred to me that Manola owed them some of her time also.

"Shall I return?" she repeated.

I hadn't faced the fact that Rachel might not return, and Manola's question pushed that matter to the forefront of my thinking. It would not be that unusual for a maid to remain in a house occupied only by a man; men of my standing normally had maids that managed their households. On the other hand, she had a family who would benefit from the attention she had devoted to my wife all this time and I realized that she was leaning in that direction.

"Will you return when my wife comes back?"

It was a question that needed to be asked, regardless of my thoughts on the reality of the issue. Manola nodded her head, and then turned to gather

her own things in the back room that served as her private space in our house.

April 1738
Venice

I visited Rachel often in the beginning, although the time spent together was difficult for me. The doctors allowed me some privacy while we visited, but that allowance was limited to about one hour each time. They would reappear after that interval and, with their application of medication and attention to Rachel's mood, indicate to me that my visit should come to an end.

"Is there still music?" she asked me soon after my arrival each time.

"Yes, there is still music," although I didn't understand the meaning of her question. I queried the doctors about this and they commented that she seemed preoccupied with music, usually speaking of the violin specifically, and that she asked about concerts in the city, and about Antonio Vivaldi often.

The man himself had become a peripatetic wanderer, moving from Venice to other cities and back again, struggling to reinvigorate his career and remind audiences of the importance of his compositions in the world of music. In my quiet moments, I admitted to myself that my wife was more impressed with Antonio's success in music than my own success in business. I also acknowledged silently that the attentions that he paid to her might have swayed her feelings about me.

He was sixty years old now and no longer the swordsman that women swooned over, but a woman whose mind lingered on the past might still harbor great love for him.

"Is there anything that I can do for you?" I asked her.

Rachel smiled at me as if she barely knew me. I had noticed over the last few visits that her memory had selected certain chapters of her life to retain, and that I was not present in those chapters.

"No, thank you sir," she replied. "But could you change the water in that vase?"

She pointed to a spot on the bedstand beside her but, when I looked, I saw no vase. Rather than quibble with her request, I simply agreed to do that.

When I exited her room, I asked the doctor about her imaginings.

"Oh, she gets a rose once in a while," he said. "It is a single bud in a little vase."

"Is there a note?"

"Just the initials A.V." He had reached the same conclusion that I had. "She is quite an admirer of his, but I am sure you know that."

"Yes, she can admire him, but the delivery of a rose to her room would require that the feeling be mutual. Wouldn't you agree?"

I shot this question at the doctor with a bit more impulse than I had intended, and he nodded lamely before turning away from me.

August 1739
Venice

I continued my visits to Rachel, who now had lived in *L'Ospedale* for three years. Her physical condition had worsened, although her mood was often imbued with a childlike quality. She would want to play little games of dice and smooth stones, and she would talk of music as if it emanated from the ceiling.

"Is there still music?" she continued to ask. By this time, I didn't want to answer because I couldn't tell whether she was talking in general about the world of music, or whether I, too, heard it from above.

"How is he?" she asked.

I flinched at the question. There had been isolated incidents of the rosebud and note, some seen directly by me and some mentioned by nursemaids in the hallway when I approached. If my wife retained only some memories of life, I wanted them to be about me not Antonio.

It was in the stifling heat of the summer that I was summoned to *L'Ospedale* by Doctor Aurelio.

"Your wife did not suffer; her derangement prevented her from knowing any true pain."

His use of the past tense startled me and I leaned back against the wall.

"I'm sorry, Signor Trapensi. I did not realize that Manola had not spoken to you. She was here this morning to collect your wife's clothing. Rachel passed away in the night. She had grown gaunt from lack of sleep and food, and her mind wandered to places that we could not know or understand.

"She spoke of you with kindness, though, sir. And she thanked you for your support, and the lessons you had given her."

Doctor Aurelio had been misled by Rachel's senseless comments. He thought that she was appreciative of some training or learning that I had provided, when I knew that the instruction that most mattered to her was in music, and it did not come from my hand.

I buried my wife the next day and returned to a house that had been deprived of her love and spirit for three years, and now would be deprived of her presence for all time. Manola was not there, of course, and I did not yet know whether I would recall her.

October 1740
Vienna

I spent most of my time at the office, a fact which disaffected Dario, I am sure. But my home was cold and unwelcoming and I saw no reason to spend my days there.

I also ceased frequenting the cafés except for my daily meals. Manola had remained with her family and I required sustenance.

Antonio was still trying to resuscitate his career and had some luck in that arena. He attracted the attention of Charles VI, the Holy Roman Emperor who resided in the Hofburg Palace in Vienna. Finally securing such an important sponsor, Antonio moved to Vienna himself and took up a residence near Kärntnertortheater. Bad luck was in store, though, and Antonio's sponsor died soon after the *maestro* relocated, on the twentieth day of October, in Seventeen Forty.

I had occasion to visit Vienna on business and saw him a few times. Antonio was poorer than I recalled from Venice, a fact which satisfied the dark urge of revenge within me. When we crossed paths, he would call out gaily though, as in old times.

"Domenico, my good friend. How are you?"

His salutation was clearly to disguise his penurious state, and I was unable to speak kindly with him. The memory of my wife's unrequited longing was still fresh in my memory. We would engage in a brief conversation and then part ways.

July 28, 1741
Late Evening, Vienna

The Trapensi business continued to grow and, with it, our market. Goods were being shipped all over Europe and I took the opportunity to accompany some of the products when the destination was the bigger cities. Immersing myself in the gaiety of places like Paris and Zurich brightened my spirits.

I also went to Vienna, but my mood was more complicated whenever I was in that city. Antonio had remained there even after his benefactor had passed from the scene. But I heard stories about how he had taken up a new residence, a cheaper apartment, according to his available funds.

This afternoon, I received a note at my apartment that Antonio was inviting me to visit him. The note gave no indication whether I was the only guest, but it called out the address of his current residence, an apartment in a small neighborhood of Vienna not known for spacious accommodations. From that, I concluded that this might be a private meeting, one that I both welcomed and dreaded.

I signed my name and acceptance at the bottom of the note and sent the messenger on his way to reply to Antonio.

When evening fell, my skin tingled and I thought I felt an unseasonable chill in the air. I walked along Kramergasse toward Stephansdom and, as I stepped around the corner of the cathedral at St. Stephen's, I felt a tickle on the exposed skin at the back of my neck. Thinking it was the bony digit of death scratching at me, I swatted the feeling away, then pulled the collar of my evening jacket up to the hairline behind my ears.

Antonio lived in a small apartment on the second floor of a building on Wollzeile, so my steps turned left onto Bradstätte and continued for a block, then right onto Wollzeile as the lights of the inns and bars blinked on. A woman with white-powdered face and lurid red lipstick waved at me from an open window above the pavement, but I ignored her greeting and continued on.

By the time I reached Antonio's apartment, night had fallen. I climbed the steps and rapped on the wooden door which he opened with alacrity, greeting me as if in old times. He invited me in and offered a chair by the fire, which I took as soon as I had doffed my hat. Antonio took up his position on the bench in front of his pianoforte. Known best for performing on the violin, the *maestro* preferred to compose new works on that keyboard, which I knew already.

Our conversation was performed as one between men of an advanced age who shared memories of life and time. A stranger standing in his doorway that evening would have thought of us as close companions, if the stranger failed to interpret the pain hidden behind my tightly pursed lips.

While we talked, Antonio's fingers kept tapping the keys of the pianoforte. Not loudly enough to interfere with our conversation, but the repetitive action still distracted me.

"Are you writing something?" I asked.

"I'm always writing something," he replied, and a distant memory flooded back to me from years past.

"Would you like to hear it?"

I nodded, as duty would require.

The melody was a lonely dirge that lifted from the lower register of piano keys as his fingers gently pressed and then slid off the edge of the ivory. He had just completed the writing of it. He didn't say it was his masterpiece, but he wanted a sign of approval from me. I smiled lightly at his plea.

After a long performance which Antonio carried out primarily to please himself – and not me – he stopped. The last notes hung in the air for a moment and I had to admit silently that it was a composition that would be long remembered by the public, if they ever heard it.

Antonio dropped his chin as if he was tired. I could hear his breathing which came in little gasps, the same raspy sounds that he had endured his entire life. He lifted his right hand to his chest and placed it lightly there, not to compress it but almost to console the muscles between his ribs and encourage them to do their job.

Without speaking to me, he rose and stepped over to the cot that served as his bed. The apartment was quite small, and he slept in the same room we now sat in, so he lowered himself onto the rumpled blanket to rest. His right hand was still on his chest and his eyes stared without purpose toward the tiled ceiling above.

After another moment I stood, but rather than moving toward the door, I walked toward the cot. Antonio glanced at me as I reached the cot and hovered over it. I gently moved his right hand off of his chest and placed it alongside of him.

I then placed my two hands on his chest, straightened my arms so that my elbows were not bent, and leaned forward.

Antonio's eyes opened wide and he reached up with both hands to grasp my wrists. I stared directly into his eyes, but I knew his strength would not be enough to counter the weight of my body pressing down on him.

I held that position, lowering my body ever so gradually until I could feel Antonio's chest giving way to my touch. Tears formed in the corners of his eyes, eyes which were still fixed on my own.

I leaned in again and gave a little jerk of my arms, compressing his ribs even more.

Antonio's raspy breathing had turned to a thin whisper, trying with little energy to draw air into his chest against the pressure I was applying.

A twitch of his hands gave away his failing spirit, and I noticed that my mouth had become twisted in anger and spite.

Another twitch and his grip loosened ever so slightly. I leaned in more and listened to his breathing, until I heard none.

I continued the pressure for several more seconds but saw the light go out of his eyes. Then I raised up, looked at him one more time, retrieved my hat and left the apartment.

October 24, 1741
Venice

I was still in Vienna after that night at Antonio's apartment and I heard the news on the street that the great composer, Antonio Vivaldi, had expired the evening before. The report indicated that his lifelong ailment of hard breathing had been his undoing, and that he was found in his apartment by the maid.

"His eyes were still open," she said, and made a little gesture of her hand as if holding back the evil that brings death to our door. "He looked like he just stopped in the middle of a thought. I hope that death claims me in such a calm manner."

The Viennese people didn't know me well, except for the businessmen of the city, but I thought it would be appropriate behavior to remain through his interment.

I witnessed the process much as the others who had gathered there. But I felt no remorse for my role in his demise; I even felt a bit of relief, a small victory over the man who had haunted my life. He excelled in music where I had failed. He paraded around with his coterie of girls while I limped along on a bad leg. And, ultimately, he stole the love my wife should have given to me.

After his burial, I quickened my pace and left Vienna as soon as I could. I wanted to return to Venice promptly; I even wondered whether at the age of sixty-three I shouldn't abandon future travel and retire to my city.

Upon my return to Venice, I went straight to the cemetery where Rachel was placed after her death two years before. I visited that place less often than I had visited her in *L'Ospedale* but I had been away for some time and I felt a particular urge to spend a moment with my wife. Antonio had been dead for several months and I had rescued myself from the moments of anger and the pangs of revenge that delivered me to his apartment, and delivered him to his grave.

There was a little frost on the ground, but the crystals were melting in the sunlight that warmed the air.

Beside the small stone that I had erected to Rachel there was a single red rose, with a slip of paper initialed A.V. The rose was fresh, certainly picked that day.

Blood rushed into my cheeks and I spun around in confusion and dismay. I couldn't tell how the rose had gotten to her gravesite, or who had delivered it for Antonio after all this time. He was dead. I knew that without a doubt.

But A.V.?

November 12, 1741
Venice

I slept fitfully for weeks after that visit to the cemetery. Antonio Vivaldi, my nemesis, was A.V., but how could a rose be delivered to Rachel's gravesite long after the musician had left this world?

This morning, I went to Manola's house to interrogate her. They lived down a narrow street in a poor quarter of Venice, respectable and clean, but without the light of the sun nor the smell of the sea, both conditions long enjoyed by my people and those of means.

When I laid my knuckles on her door, it opened after only a single knock. Manola stood there and her husband, a rugged man of the sea stood behind her.

"May I ask you some questions?"

"Yes, sire," was her reply, but she pushed her two little children back from the encounter and came outside the house to speak with me.

"Who is A.V.?"

Manola looked directly at me, leaving no doubt that she had anticipated this visit and knew exactly what my purpose was in the visit.

"Those are Antonio Vivaldi's letters," she said firmly. She knew, as did I, that she was being evasive and she probably also knew that the delaying tactic would not be tolerated by me for very long.

"Who is A.V.?" I repeated.

Manola looked down at her feet and then muttered, "Arturo Visetti."

My head began to spin, and then the whole world around me joined in. I felt my lips forming words but no sound came. A pain appeared in my head and shot arrows down my spine. My stomach began to convulse and a bilious smell rose in my throat.

I leaned back but found nothing to support me. As my legs staggered I stared at Manola who stood resolutely with her hands clasped at her waist, staring at me but offering no support for my sudden fit of dizziness.

When I regained some balance and my senses began to return, I heard faint sounds coming from my mouth, as if I was outside of my own body and witnessing some wretched scene from a distance.

"Who is Visetti?"

"He is a minor musician who thought he could play violin," Manola replied with little emotion. "His skill never equaled his wishes, and he remained in the background at the *Conservatorio*, consigned to help with the school but not sufficient to take instruction."

"Did my wife know him?"

It was a direct question with little room for evasion, but Manola seemed not a bit put off by it. Perhaps she had less respect for me than I had imagined all these years, and now her situation allowed her to advance her thoughts without fear of repercussions.

"Yes, he knew her. He was in love with her."

"And Rachel?"

"Rachel never bore any children with you," she began slowly, staring into my eyes. "But she never bore any children by Visetti, either."

What Manola didn't say bothered me very much. She never bore children by him, but that didn't mean she didn't give him her love.

"Why did she die?" I asked.

Manola thought for a moment.

"Old men should not marry young girls," she replied. Then she turned abruptly and disappeared into her home.

My beloved Rachel is dead, and possibly broken hearted before the end came. I had killed the greatest musician of our time. And a man who stole my wife from me was still at large, still loving my wife with his little roses and notes.

I couldn't kill again. Oh, I certainly had murder in mind, but my last act of revenge had gone terribly wrong. I got away with it, but could I repeat my luck if I confronted this Arturo Visetti? And could an old man with a gimpy leg overpower a man many years his junior.

My days are now spent in my office more than at home. I released Dario, encouraging him to find other work, and now I am responsible for the lonely task of carrying on a family business with no family to carry it on for.

About the Author

D.P. Rosano's travels around the world always come back to Italy, where the art and culture of the land define the lives and livelihood of the people there.

D.P. Rosano has managed these travels under a nom de guerre, fighting terrorists and criminal gangs while passing through society as a wine and food critic. The duality of D.P.'s life is brought forth in these novels, merging the aromas of food with the sights and sounds of Italy, to portray the colorful history of the land through the personalities and culture of the people.

Books by the Author

A Love Lost in Positano
To Rome, With Love

Lightning Source UK Ltd.
Milton Keynes UK
UKHW010916271120
374179UK00001B/106